Padre Porko

The Gentlemanly Pig

By

ROBERT DAVIS

Illustrated by
Fritz Eichenberg

HOLIDAY HOUSE

BY THE SAME AUTHOR

PEPPERFOOT OF THURSDAY MARKET
HUDSON BAY EXPRESS
GID GRANGER
PARTNERS OF POWDER HOLE
THAT GIRL OF PIERRE'S

Foreword

IN *Guide of Southern Spain,* edited by Muirhead, reference is made to earliest carvings in stone, nearly obliterated by time, but of *undoubtedly porcine character.* These must antedate the Moorish occupation, as the Mohammedan considered swine unclean. They may even go back beyond the Visigoth and the Roman, to the original Iberic stock, which was Celtic. In Celtic regions the pig is much valued, and is the most important domestic animal. It harmonizes with what we know of Celtic character that there should be a legendary figure of a wise and benevolent spirit, in the form of a pig.

The first time I heard the words "Padre Porko" was from a doctor in Cadiz. Referring to a matter which had escaped our control, he remarked, "We'll have to leave it to Padre Porko." It had the same significance as though an American had said, "We'll have to trust to luck." Without quite remanding the affair to Providence, it yet indicated that a spiritual force, not unfriendly, became responsible.

In the winter of 1938 means of communication were demoralized in Spain. I was able to assist an elderly lady who was searching for one of her daughters. For forty-eight hours we were fellow-passengers in an overcrowded and dilatory train. This lady had all the Celt's imagination, had lived in the country districts, and herself brought up a large family. She had a great fund of local superstitions and customs, and the legends and fables that children love. By the end of that journey the character and many of the genial exploits of the fabulous pig were distinct in my mind. The main elements of this incongruous fairy were his ability to talk all languages, his humorous good sense, and his belief that all animals could and should work together. She was to the Padre what Uncle Remus was to Br'er Rabbit. I have not seen the lady again, nor did she give me her name. But the tales of the Padre come from a background which is authentic, and the central figure can honestly be believed to have its origins in a far distant past.

Robert Davis

Contents

PADRE PORKO
The Gentlemanly Pig

*I*t was eight o'clock. A few pale stars were hanging out their lamps. The supper of white cheese, salt and bread, washed down with warm goat's milk, had been eaten. The girls had washed the bowls at the spring and had smoothed the blankets over the straw to make the beds. The boys had piled brush wood to dry for the morning's fire, and had driven the goats in under the severe eye of the sheep-dog.

Inside there was no light but the blaze of the fire. Baby Micas and three-year-old Alfonso were already dreaming. Other young figures lay motionless upon the straw. Grandmother Freitas sat with her head leaning against the wall. But the older children, although silent, were far from sleep. A *hundred exciting thoughts raced through their heads. Their eyes were open, staring at the ceiling. A sugary voice broke the quiet darkness. It was Manolo, the oldest boy, asking a favor of his grandmother.*

"Granny Maria, our dear, darling Avuelita Maria, here are your grandchildren, who adore and salute you with respect. Do you not find it in your heart to tell us a tale? A tale of that knightly gentleman of the old Spain, the Padre Porko. We younger ones hunger to know the wisdom and the laughter that he brought to our land. And who can tell of him like yourself?"

Half-awake, other small voices joined Manolo. "Please, Oh please, Avuelita Maria! Tell us one story, no more than one, and we shall sleep, not moving an eyelash, until the sky is red again."

By the fire the slight body of Doña Maria Freitas stirred. Her bird-like fingers opened and closed upon the handle of her walking-stick. She folded the shawl back from her forehead and spoke, hardly louder than the whispering of the wind.

"Once, long ago, the men knew less and the animals knew more. Everything that moved and breathed lived together as one family. The ruler of the man tribe was the king. The ruler of the animals was the Padre Porko. But both the king and the Padre Porko wanted all beings, from the biggest to the smallest, to feel like brothers toward one another. This was very long ago.

" The Padre came to Spain with the Irish, hundreds of years before the Romans and the Arabs, and such quarrelsome people. He loved our beautiful wide plains, the clear air of the hills, our swift rivers, our sunny valleys, our forests of oak and pine, the ocean that pounds on its shore. And the good Padre has lived with us ever since, as the best friend of every Spaniard.

"My great-grandmother knew an old man who, when a boy, saw the Padre, just for a moment, in an orchard of olive trees, by the light of a new

moon. *He is all pink, like a baby that has been scrubbed in hot water. He wears a green velvet jacket with gold buttons, and green velvet pantaloons, a red beret on his head and red slippers on his feet.*

"Somewhere in the far-away hills the Padre has a neat green house, in the center of a vegetable garden. In front of his door grows an umbrella pine, in the shade of which the Padre has a table and chair, where he sits in pleasant weather. An old lady hedge-hog keeps house for him. She sweeps up the ashes, cooks his porridge and his soup of carrots and turnips, and takes care of his four hives of bees. For you must know that while the Padre is the friend of everybody, what he really loves, with the appetite of a truly piggy person, is honey and stewed carrots.

"But any Spanish boy or girl or animal, who really needs the Padre's help, can have it. If you are in bad trouble all you need do is to go to a

quiet place, and wish for him terribly hard. Say, inside your own heart, 'Padre, Padre, I do not know what to do, and you must come. Please come, I am waiting.' He will be there, never fear. Everything that lives will carry him your message: the wasps and the bees, the moles and the bats, the birds and the foxes. They are all his friends, and when you call him they become your friends.

"And you, small and much-loved children of my sons, if you work and are obedient, if you do the things that must be done for comfort and neatness, each evening, when the supper is eaten and the fire burns low, I will tell you a tale of that great caballero of our land, the Padre Porko."

"I, Maria, tell to my grandchildren what Maria, my grandmother, heard from her grandmother, Maria."

The General's *HORSE*

*J*t was a misty-moisty evening. The drops of rain fell from the tips of the leaves, with a "plop," into the puddles underneath. The wind blew the branches of the umbrella pine against the windows of the Padre's house. It was the sort of weather when no person or animal was willingly out-of-doors. The honest creatures of the air, the forest and the earth had long been asleep.

The Widow Hedge-Hog had washed the supper dishes, swept the hearth with her tail, warmed the Padre's flannel pajamas, and gone home to her family under the apple tree.

Before his fire the Padre dozed. He had eaten three plates of heavenly stewed carrots for his supper, and every now and then he rubbed his stomach gently, to help them digest. The tapping of the branches on the window and the falling of the rain made a soothing music. Upon the shelf above the chimney stood a polished red apple. The Padre was trying to decide whether he should eat the apple or smoke his pipe before crawling into bed for a good night's sleep.

"Rat-a-tat-tat-tat," suddenly sounded the knocker on his door.

"My Goodness Gracious," he exclaimed, pushing his feet into his red slippers. "Who can be out on a night like this? It must be someone in real trouble."

"Who is there?" he called, putting his sensitive nose to the keyhole. He could learn more through his nose than many people can learn through their ears and eyes.

"It is Antonio, the stable-boy from the General's."

"Come in, come in," invited the Padre, seating himself again, and taking out his pipe.

The door opened and a dripping figure stepped inside. Very politely he waited on the door-mat, his cap in his hand.

"Your Honor will please to excuse me for coming so late," he said. "But it was only to-night that the General said he would send me away in disgrace. My Grandmother told me that Your Honor is the Godfather of all Spanish boys who do not have real fathers, so you will please to excuse my coming."

The Padre was reaching up for the red apple. "She told you the truth, Antonio. You sit here and eat this apple, while I put tobacco in my pipe." With a skillful movement of his left hind foot the Padre kicked dry branches upon the fire.

"And don't be in any hurry, Antonio. Take all the time you need. Tell me the very worst. Whatever the trouble, we can put it right."

"It is about the white horse," Antonio began, "the fat, white one, that the General rides in parades, at the head of his soldiers. He can't walk. It is his left front hoof." The boy gulped it out in a single breath.

"They say that it is my fault, that I made him fall when I rode him for exercise. But it's not true. I always go slowly, and turn corners at a walk."

"Let's go and see," said the Padre, going to the closet for his rubber coat. "And here's a cape for you to put around your shoulders."

Once at the General's, the Padre and Antonio hung their wet things in the harness-room and unhooked the door of the box stall where the white horse lived. He was a superb animal, but he stood with one front foot off the floor.

"Excuse me, Your Excellency," said the Padre, "but can you tell me the cause of Your Excellency's lameness?"

The great beast pricked up his ears. "The cause of it!" he snorted. "Why a three-day-old colt would know that much, and yet these stupid doctors and professors have been pestering me for two weeks. A wire nail has gone into the tender center of my foot. It has no head. You cannot see it. The idiots, and they pretend to know so much."

"I thought as much," murmured the Padre, sympathetically. "And will Your Excellency co-operate with us, if we try to get the nail out?"

"Won't I, though!" The horse snorted again. "Why, I haven't been able to touch this foot to the ground for sixteen days."

"This is a case for the Rat Family, and for no one else," said the Padre to himself. He trotted over to a hole in the stable floor. His voice, as he leaned over the opening, was a soft whine through his nose. "Is the lady of the house at home?"

A gray muzzle appeared. "I am only a poor widow, Don Porko; my husband was caught in a trap last harvest time. But if my children and a poor soul like me can be of any help to you, you are more than welcome to our best."

"Indeed you can, Mrs. Furrynose," said the Padre with enthusiasm. "We animals are going to do what none of the veterinary professors knew how to do. Listen carefully. Of all the rats in this town which one has the strongest teeth?" Other heads had joined Mother Furrynose at the opening, and now they all answered in a single unanimous squeak, "Uncle Israel, down at the flour-mill."

"Good," said the Padre. "And now, Mrs. Furrynose, I want you to listen once more. Will you send your oldest boy for Uncle Israel right away? Tell him that Padre Porko needs all the husky boy and girl rats in this town at the General's stable in half-an-hour."

Before the Padre had finished his request, a

sleek rat was out of the hole and running toward the door. "You can count on us, Chief," he called.

Hardly ten minutes had passed when a peculiar noise was heard outside the stable. It was like the wind blowing the dry leaves in October. It was a rustling, a bustling, a scratching, a scraping, a marching of countless feet. Uncle Israel entered at the head of his tribe. He was an old-fashioned Quaker rat, gray and gaunt, and the size of a half-grown kitten. When he smiled he showed his remarkable teeth, sharp as razors and the color of ivory. He motioned to his brown-coated army and they lined up in rows around the wall, watching him and the Padre with shoe-button eyes.

"I'm not so strong as I used to be," apologized Uncle Israel, "except for my teeth. I don't want to boast, but none of these young rats can hold on to things as hard as I can. As soon as I got your message I brought my relatives.

We will do anything you say, Padre." The rows of heads nodded in agreement.

"Thank you for coming, Uncle Israel," said the Padre. "In a minute I'll explain what our work is going to be. First we must tell the General's horse our plan."

He stood by the shoulder of the white horse and spoke in his most persuasive way. "Your Excellency, we are ready for the operation that will cure your foot. But we must be sure of your co-operation. It may hurt, I'm afraid, especially at first."

"It can't hurt more than my hoof aches right now. Go ahead," said the horse.

"We must uncover the end of the nail so that Uncle Israel can grip it in his beautiful teeth. Please bend back your foot."

The General's horse rested his foot on the straw, with the under side showing, and Uncle Israel, placing one paw on either edge of the tender V, began to gnaw, his teeth cutting in like a machine. Presently he sat up, squeaking excitedly. "I have it. It's right there. It's like a piece of wire. But I can get a good hold on it. What next, Padre?"

"Antonio," ordered the Padre, "bring the halters that hang in the harness room, and tie the ropes one to the other. And you, Uncle Israel, slip your head through this loop in the leather. We will run the long rope out across the stable floor so that everyone can find a hold. Take your time, Uncle Israel, everything depends upon your teeth. When you are ready for us to pull, wiggle your tail."

Things worked like clock-work. Uncle Israel held on. Three hundred young rats strained and pulled on the rope. The General's horse winced with the pain. The Padre walked up and down like a captain in a battle. But the nail in the foot of the white horse did not budge.

Padre Porko had an idea. "Widow Furrynose, what would give you the most pleasure in the world?"

The lady replied quickly. "To bury that deceitful black cat up at the miller's." Everybody sat up and clapped his paws.

"Well, young people," said the Padre, "think that you are pulling the hearse to the graveyard, and that the miller's black cat is in it. Wouldn't you manage to get that hearse to the graveyard? Pull like that."

The floor of the barn seemed alive. It was a rippling, gray-brown carpet of straining small bodies. The teeth of Uncle Israel were locked in a death grip. Padre Porko walked back and forth, singing, "Horrible cat, get her buried, haul the hearse."

And, inch by inch, a long, thin, villainous nail came out of the horse's foot.

Then what a racket! Everyone was squirm-

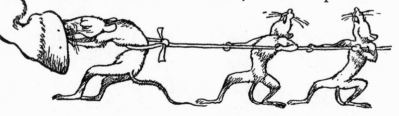

ing, and squeaking, and jumping and rolling over, and tick- ling and nipping tails, and tell- ing how strong he was. The white horse and Antonio admired Uncle Israel's teeth. And all of his nephews and nieces and grandchildren were so proud of him that they kissed him on both whiskers. Padre Porko kept repeating, "I'm proud of you. Great work! I always say that we animals can do anything, if we will work together."

But it was the General's horse who brought the evening to its perfect close. He whinnied into the Padre's ear, "Please translate to An- tonio that if he will unlock the oat box I'm

sure our friends would enjoy a light lunch. The
General himself would be the first to propose
it. He will be very thankful when he visits the
stable tomorrow and finds me trotting on four
legs."

Mrs. Furrynose and Uncle Israel had the
young people sit in circles of ten, while Antonio passed the refreshments, pouring a little
pile of oats in the center of each circle. Over
three hundred guests were served but their
table manners were excellent. No one snatched
or grabbed, or gobbled his food. Everyone said,
"If you please," and "Thank you," and "Excuse me for talking when my mouth is full."

When the crunching was at its height, Uncle
Israel made a speech. "Padre Porko, Your Excellency, and friends, relatives and neighbors,
this is a proud and happy night for me. In
all my life my teeth never did such good work
before. They helped this noble white horse,
and they enabled us rats to aid the Padre in

one of his kind acts. But, also, tonight, my teeth brought me to the attention of a lovely lady, Madame Furrynose, and I am delighted to say that she will not be a widow much longer. One and all, you are invited to the wedding, which will be held next Sunday afternoon in the flour-mill, while the miller is at church. And the Padre Porko has promised to send word to all dogs and cats of the town that none of our  guests are to be caught while going, coming or at the party." A hurricane of cheers and clapping followed the speech.

The pink nose of the white horse pushed through the window of his stall, and the merrymakers looked up. "May I, too, offer a wedding present to these worthy friends? Every night I will leave a handful of grain in the corner of my manger. They will find it there for their midnight lunch. A wedded pair with such polite manners can be trusted not to disturb the repose of a hard-working old horse."

The morning sun crept along the stable wall until it shone directly upon the sleeping Antonio. He sat up and rubbed his eyes. How did it happen that he was not in his bed, but in the box stall of the General's horse? And the horse was stamping with the foot that had been lame. Queerer still, the grain box was open and half the oats were gone. And what was the meaning of the four halter ropes tied together?

These are questions which Antonio never could answer. But when he told this story to his children, he was no longer a stable boy. He was the head trainer of all the General's racing horses.

Celestina's Silver
COFFEE-POT

ll her life Celestina had been losing things, but this was the worst of all—to have lost the Admiral's coffee-pot. She sat on her doorstep, hugging her knees, and sobbing, "The evil eye is on me, truly the evil eye is upon me."

In a way it was her own fault. She had been stupid to be so terrified. She should have marked the tree where she buried it. But the night was dark and wet. The Good-wife Maceira had rushed in without warning, crying that the soldiers were killing people in the next village. She had said that the glow in the sky was the flames of that village. She said that they must run if they would save their lives.

Celestina had snatched up the Admiral's pot, wrapped it in the apron that she was wearing, seized a spade, run out into the rainy garden, and buried it at the foot of a tree. She thought it was a peach tree—but it might have been a plum.

Not till three days later did she learn that it had all been a false alarm. There were no soldiers within fifty miles, and the glow in the sky had been Farmer Edwardo's strawstack, set on fire by mischievous boys.

But the silver pot was not to be found. For two whole days Celestina had dug and dug. Not only around peach trees and plum trees, but around every tree in the garden. Yet never a sign of apron or coffee-pot. It was no wonder that the distracted woman, her back lame from digging, her hands blistered from the shovel, and her heart heavy because of her loss, sat hugging her thin knees and sobbing at the entry of her cottage.

In their nest, over the doorway, the African swallows could not help hearing the sounds of grief. "I can't stand this any longer," snapped the husband; "it's getting on my nerves."

"Why don't you do something?" said his wife. "We have spent four seasons here, and never had a cross word from her. If I were a man, *I* would do something!"

"I will," said the African swallow.

Without being really awake, the Padre brought one of his feet from under the warm blankets and loosened the string of his nightcap. It had been too tight under his third chin. His pink, piggy face relaxed into a smile, and he snuggled back under the covers for a last snooze. Out-of-doors, the stars were growing dim in the sky, but it would be a full two hours before the Widow Hedge-Hog would have his porridge on the table. He smoothed the wrinkles out of his pajamas and within thirty seconds was snoring gently.

"Tick-Tick-Tick-Tick-Tick." The noise was not loud, but it did not stop.

The Padre's snore ended in a gurgle. He sat up, sleepily. "Bless my stars and collar buttons!" he exclaimed; "I must have a visitor." He raised the curtain and opened the window. A red-capped swallow stepped across the sill.

"If it isn't my old friend, Fernando Ruddy from Africa," said the Padre, slipping under the bedclothes again. "What brings you out so early, Fernando? Any dispute in the nest?"

"It is Celestina," said the swallow, balancing himself on the back of the Padre's red chair, "and her silver coffee-pot. She will drive us all crazy, if it isn't found. From morning till night she sits under my nest, making funny noises, with water running out of her eyes. I haven't had a real sleep for four nights."

The swallow flew across to the foot-board of the bed. "I have a very confidential idea. Haven't even told my wife. But I think . . ." For several minutes they talked in whispers.

The Padre again jumped out of bed to let his caller out. "It was perfectly fine of you to tell me about this," he thanked Fernando. "Now don't forget to have somebody find where the Owl is sleeping, and to send me word before eight o'clock. My regards to the family." The Padre thereupon slept, without a movement, a thought, or a dream, until the Widow Hedge-Hog brought his shaving water.

He dressed with care, brushing the last speck of dust from his velvet breeches, and polishing the gold buttons. And he made such a fuss over a spot on his shirt that the Widow Hedge-Hog curled up into a ball, saying, "I'm going to play dead until this man is out of the house. I think he is secretly getting married today."

The Padre leaned back in his chair and laughed. "No, no. But I am calling on a lady."

He was scraping the last drop of porridge out of the bowl when a crow called from the umbrella pine, "The Policeman of the Night sleeps today in the crooked oak, where the three roads meet." The Padre ran to the door, waving his thanks to the messenger. "This doesn't look as though it would be a difficult case," he hummed to himself.

While he dressed he had made up a new song. While buttoning his waistcoat he tried it:

> The turnip is a scrumptious fruit,
> Either cooked or raw,
> And a cauliflower in gravy
> Puts strength into your paw.
> But of the gifts that nature sends,
> In summer, spring or fall,
> A carrot stewed in buttermilk
> Is truly best of all.

Once at the great oak, where the up-hill and down-hill paths cross, he peered up into the foliage. His voice sounded like the wind blowing under a door, or down a chimney.

"Oo-oo-oo-vv-o-v-oo, Policeman of the Night, are you there?" The unseeing eyes of an Owl appeared within the crack in the hollow tree. "Indeed I am, Chief. I would have come to your house, but in sunlight like this I can see nothing."

"Sergeant, I want you to think back to the night when Farmer Edwardo's straw pile burned. Do you remember that night?"

"I should think I do. I caught seven fat field-mice running from the fire. I shall not forget that feast in a hurry."

"Now think carefully, Sergeant, did you see anyone digging in a garden that night?"

"Digging in a garden? Why, it was raining and pitch-dark. Who would be gardening on a night like that? But wait a second." The Owl

was remembering something. "Digging in a garden? Ah, now I have it. But it was not the night of Edwardo's fire, it was only three nights ago. It was the Good - wife Maceira among her grapevines, at the further end. There was a race riot at the frog-pond that night and I was on my way to make an arrest, so that I couldn't stop."

"Thank you, Policeman of the Night, thank you kindly. You have told me just what I wanted to know," said the Padre. As he trotted towards the homes of Celestina and her neighbor, his sharp little eyes were examining the roadway closely. He was looking for a track in the white dust. At length, with a grunt of satisfaction, he bent over a faint line. It was as though someone had drawn a twig across the road. "It looks like the Old Judge himself," said the Padre, "and he passed only a few minutes ago, for no one has mussed up his track."

Beyond the highway, to the left, was a pile of loose rocks. The Padre halted some fifteen feet from it. He was taking no chances with the uncertain disposition of a sleeping stone-snake. His voice, when he spoke, was through his nose, like the buzzing of a hive of bees.

"I salute the Honorable Judge Fork-Tongue." He cocked his head and listened. Three times he was obliged to repeat. "I guess the Judge is lying on his good ear," he muttered, taking a deep breath and making a noise that sounded like a thousand bumble-bees.

A sleepy hiss came from behind the rocks. Encouraged by the reply the Padre said, "Honorable Judge, I take the liberty of asking where the deep-digger moles are at present working."

"Go away. Let me sleep. Let me sleep. Among the cedar trees on the hill of the Yellow Flowers. Let me sleep. Go away."

The Padre smiled pleasantly. He knew what he needed to know. "A thousand thanks, my dear Judge Fork-Tongue, and if ever Padre Porko can serve you and your people, you have only to send me the signal."

A stone at the top of the pile seemed to shiver upon its base, as coils of gray-blue rope came slithering from under it. An eight foot rock-snake had boiled up from nowhere. A blunt triangle of a head, with cold eyes, was lifted to the Padre's middle button.

"My dear Colleague and Chief," hissed the Judge. "I never dreamed it was you. I was taking thirty winks. What was it you were saying about the digger-moles?"

"I want six of their best workmen, at the valley side of the Good-wife Maceira's garden, when the sun casts no shadow," replied the Padre.

Judge Fork-Tongue undulated to a flat stone, raised about two feet of his tail into the air and brought it down on the rock with a dry, wooden slap. Four times he did this. All up the hillside from the stone walls and the tree roots, the Padre could see pieces of steel-gray woolen yarn, eddying towards the Judge. His tribe was answering their President's signal. "You can count on having your six workmen, Padre. And if they don't give satisfaction, my family will have them all eaten and digested before Saturday night."

The Padre continued on his way to the Good-wife's garden and had a nice little nap while awaiting the moles. It was considerate of Judge Fork-Tongue to bring the workmen himself, on his broad, wide back, but it was distressing for the moles. The Padre laughed when he saw them leaning over the edge, and being sea-sick.

"Excuse us for a moment," they said, rolling to the ground. "It was good of the Judge to bring us, but we prefer to go home under ground, by ourselves. You cannot imagine such an unwholesome motion, like a small boat in a hurricane." The Padre laughed again and the Judge laughed with him and in ten minutes the deep-digger moles felt enough recovered to laugh a little, too.

"Now, what I want of you boys," explained the Padre, "is to find a metal object that is buried in this garden. It belongs to a friend of mine, who is a good friend of all the animals. It is among the grapevines, at the other end, and not very deep, not deeper than twenty or twenty-five paws. I suggest that we divide that corner of the vines into six equal parts. The Judge, who likes arithmetic, will use his body as a tape measure. And then each of you can burrow back and forth until we discover the silver coffee-pot. Now, let's get below ground."

The deep-digger mole has a nose like a snow-plow. His hind legs are built to push the nose forward, and his front legs are shaped like trowels, to clear the earth from under his nose. His front legs work like a boy swimming dog-paddle in the water. Among all the animals there has never been a tunnel-maker who could travel so fast, underground, as a two-year-old deep-digger mole. The six of them, who had come on the Judge's back, disappeared from view in a cascade of flying garden soil. They were specialists in deep-dirt-diving.

It seemed like no time at all, until one of the diggers pushed his snow-plow nose into the air.

"The coffee-pot is right here, Padre. As a matter of fact my hind foot is touching it."

"Bully for you, my brave Pluto," cried the Padre. "Judge Fork-Tongue, call in the other workers; the pot is found!" And, taking off his coat, the Padre began to make the soft earth fly with his own pink trotters.

Within five minutes the Admiral's coffee-pot, still wrapped in Celestina's apron, was safe under the Padre's arm, the six digger-moles were in his pockets, and, with Judge Fork-Tongue flowing easily alongside, they were headed for the cottage of Celestina.

The Padre paused before the door, and set the moles carefully on the ground. "As you boys don't like riding on the Judge's back and as it is getting late, I'm going to borrow Celestina's dog to carry you to the hill of the Yellow Flowers in this basket. Take the handle in your mouth, Lolita, and don't gallop or jolt the passengers. Set them down at the foot of the big cedar. At the new moon I shall see all of you good people at the Animals' Meeting, and will tell what fine work you have done today. Until then, please accept my sincere thanks." The white dog trotted off proudly.

The Padre, still with the apron and its precious contents under his arm, approached the cottage door. The African swallows, looking down from their nest, could hardly sit still.

"Have you got it?" chirped Fernando. Inside the house the sobs of Celestina could be heard. The poor woman was quite worn out.

The Padre laid his bundle on the table and coughed twice. Celestina raised her head. "Senorita," he said, respectfully holding his beret in his hand, "I have the honor to inform you that your swallows have brought you good fortune. Kindly observe what is on the table."

Celestina turned the silver pot round and round. She could not believe her eyes. Then she commenced to talk. "How can I ever repay you? How did you know it was lost? You are the most wonderful, handsome, intelligent, and charming animal on this earth, Don Porko. Here is my pocket-book; take what is in it."

"If you want me to speak frankly, Honorable Lady," said the Padre, "what I would most enjoy would be a few of the luscious turnips that are growing just inside your garden. To me they are worth more than diamonds."

"Take as many as you like, the whole garden is yours," cried Celestina.

The Padre retired with a bow. And as he threw the lavender and white vegetables into his bag, he made up another song.

His red beret was tilted over one ear, and his voice was clear and carefree when he trotted out of Celestina's garden into the high-road, the bulging sack over his shoulder. As he sang he would take a skippy little dance step to the right, and then another skip to the left.

A DOG Who Talked

A fish-eagle, who of all the sky people can see the farthest, glided down out of the blue, in wide slow circles. He perched upon the top branch of a pear tree, folded his steel-gray wings, and called a hoarse "Good fishing, Don Porko." The workman among the carrots hitched his suspenders higher upon his sloping shoulders and wiped the moisture from his pink forehead.

"You are far from the seashore, King of the Fishermen," said the Padre.

"I have run away from my duty of catching sardines for the greediest baby eagles in the world," replied the bird, "to bring you a message. On the western slope of Camel's Hump

Mountain a shepherd calls for you. Salvatore is his name. He lives beside the twin oaks."

The Padre buttoned his slippers and told Madame Hedge-Hog that he would be away for lunch. "I know the man. I go." The eagle jumped into the air, tucked his yellow legs inside his feathers and soared seaward.

Salvatore and his dog, Fidele, were so occupied with one another that they did not notice the Padre's approach. The shepherd was seated, and the dog was resting her chin upon his knee. She was trying to tell him something. A soft voice spoke beside them.

"My friends, you have wanted the Padre Porko?"

"I cannot stand it, I am so lonely," said the old man. "Since my wife died and my children have moved to the town I have no one to talk to. In the morning I wake, and there is no one. At noon I sit to eat, and there is no one to converse with. In the evening I smoke beside my chimney, and there is no voice to listen to. Never any sound but the rain, the wind, the bleating of the sheep. I shall become crazy with lonesomeness.

"This dog here, Fidele, knows more than many a person," the shepherd went on. "About sheep and the weather she knows everything. She wishes to talk with me. Would you, good Padre, teach this dog to speak with a man's tongue? You know every language. Give her the knowledge of saying words. I will give you a fat lamb every week, if you will. Most humbly I ask that you do this good act." The man's hand trembled with eagerness.

"It will depend upon Fidele," replied the Padre. "It is a long labor to change the form of a dog's throat. But it can be done, if she wills to make the effort. I will ask her."

The Padre explained to the dog that he would give her a lesson each morning and each night, but that through the day she would need to practice the new sounds, to say them over, thousands of times, until her lips and tongue learned to move in a different way. Fidele promised to do her part. She was clever, obedient and loyal. "He makes foolish mistakes and many of them," she confided. "I could manage the farm much better than the shepherd does." It was therefore agreed. Fidele gave her master's hand an affectionate lick, and left at the heels of her new professor.

Having spent her life among men and sheep, the dog knew the meaning of many common words. The difficulty was that she, herself, had never tried to pronounce these sounds. But the Padre was patient, and as soon as her throat was able to form the sounds, she began building short sentences.

After two months of tiresome work, the Padre patted Fidele's head one morning and said, "Old dog, you have learned all that you can from me. The rest will come from actual talking. Talk with as many people as you can, use new words, pronounce them slowly. Salvatore will have found your absence long, I fear. Do you think that you can find your way home all by yourself?"

"Why of course I can." Fidele drew back her lips in what she believed to be a genial smile. But if you had not known that it was a smile, you would have thought that she was baring her long teeth to jump at your throat. "I know the road to the ford of the river, and from that point one can see the twin oaks beside our cabin. No one will ever catch me."

The Widow Hedge-Hog had wrapped a nice lunch of johnny-bread in rhubarb leaves, and she and the Padre waved goodby to the educated dog. She went gaily along, tail in the air, practicing the speech in man's language that she would make to Salvatore. Nor did she forget the Padre's advice, to talk as much as she could, and with many people, to improve her accent. If she met strangers on the road she would exchange a few courteous sentences. The lunch, which she carried in her mouth, interfered with her vocal exercises, so she ate it, and then felt even more content with the universe.

Traveling in the same direction, Fidele spied a stout woman upon a donkey. Two baskets contained the ducks and eggs that she was taking to market. "We will have a nice chat," thought Fidele with pleasure, "as we go along, side by side. Probably we are both mothers, and she may enjoy hearing how I nursed twelve babies at the same time."

On her cushioned feet the dog was beside the donkey before the fat woman noticed her. Fidele uncovered her teeth, in one of her blood-curdling expressions of good will. "Good morning, dear lady," she said. The woman's eyes opened wide in horror. She turned white. Her jaw wagged up and down, but no sound came. Without warning, she rolled backward off the donkey and lay, quivering, in a pool of mud.

"She is afraid of something," reflected the dog. Standing over the stout body, and being careful of her accent, she said distinctly, "I am here to help you. I am your friend."

A moan shook the woman. "I am dead, dead, and this the devil himself. Go away, devil, go away. Take my donkey, take my pocketbook, but go away."

Fidele did not understand. The woman might be sick. Perhaps she disliked that particular donkey. "Do you mean to say that you give me the ducks and the donkey?" she asked.

"Yes, a thousand times, yes. Take them but leave me. Oh, that they should have sent the devil himself to get me! Go, go."

Anxious to oblige, as always, Fidele took the halter in her mouth and led the loaded donkey away. "It's queer that she didn't wish to practice talking with me. I'm sure that I spoke correctly." The woman was sitting up by now, and screaming for help from Heaven.

Fidele realized that she had received a very rich present, but the donkey could not trot fast, and it was noon before they reached the crossing of the river. There they saw a band of gypsies encamped in the shade, and around them the wagons in which they lived. Fidele had always liked gypsies; in fact, her first husband had been one. Confident of a warm welcome, and proud of her donkey, she approached the camp. She was still at some distance when a boy jumped up from the circle around the fire, and snatched the halter from her mouth. "See what I've got, see what I've got," he shouted, counting the ducks.

"Excuse me," said Fidele, "the donkey is mine. He was given me by a lady."

The boy stood, petrified with astonishment.

"The dog talks," he shrieked. "She talks!"

A bony old woman near the fire cried, "She is a ghost, don't touch her. Don't touch the donkey either. They will put a curse on you."

The leader of the band had joined the boy. "So you can talk, can you?" he said roughly, coming close to the dog.

"A little. I am beginning," answered Fidele, glad to be spoken to.

"Where did you steal that donkey, you thief?" With lightning quickness the hands of the man fastened about Fidele's throat from above. She could not defend herself. Struggling, he carried her to one of the house-wagons, hurled her inside, and slammed the door. And as he fastened the bolt, he sneered,

"You will not steal any ducks and donkeys in there, my handsome one."

In all her uneventful life, as the guardian of sheep, and the companion of a silent old mountaineer, Fidele had never been so scared and so angry. People were unfair. She had done no wrong. She only wanted to practice talking and be friends. Yet everyone treated her like an outlaw.

The wagon in which she found herself had a number of rolled-up mattresses piled at the rear end. The door was too solid to be broken, but there was a window. By jumping upon the mattresses she could see through it and could hear what was being said in the circle about the fire.

"What will you do with her?" the bony old woman was asking the head-man.

"There are two ways I can get money out of her," the leader replied slowly. "I shall tell the police, and get a reward from the owner

of the ducks and the donkey; also I will tell
the bishop that she is a witch, and they will
burn her, and give me the money for telling.
I go now to the town to find the ones who will
pay me."

Poor Fidele felt as good as dead already.
With people so ready to believe everything
evil about her, what chance had she of escape?
The single ray of hope was the sight of a sen-
sible-looking shepherd dog stretched on the
ground just below her window. Fidele thought
that there was an encouraging twinkle in his
eye.

"Are you all right, Madame Stranger?" the
gypsy dog inquired.

"Yes, but I must get out before the bearded
man comes back. He wants to have me killed.
Can you open the door?"

"No, it is locked. But I have a plan. Under
the mattress is a hammer. I will go down the
stream and bark as though I had a fox cornered.

The women and children will all run to see the battle. You bite the hammer hard in the middle of the handle. Climb upon the mattresses. Swing the hammer with all the strength in your neck. You can break the glass. The people will be too far away to hear. I have untied your donkey. He is beside the river with a stone on the rope. If they use me to track you I will lead them the wrong way. Good courage and a safe journey, Madame Stranger."

The gypsy dog was gone before Fidele could thank him. She found the hammer and climbed to the top of the mattresses. Shortly there was a furious barking outside the camp. The children and their mothers dropped their work and ran to save the fox skin.

With all her might Fidele swung the hammer. The glass cracked, but it took several minutes to chip away the pieces. Lightly she leaped to the ground, found her donkey, and pushed the stone from the halter. Not once did she look back. Still trembling from her narrow escape, her courage returned with the fresh air and exercise. She met but one other traveler. Scenting him long before he saw her, she hid the donkey and herself until he had passed.

Now she quit the main path and struck across the fields to a ravine that led to her master's cabin. Daylight was almost ended when her paws felt the warm dust where the sheep had been grazing that afternoon. Everything was just as she had pictured it a hundred times.

Salvatore was having an impossible time herding the playful young lambs inside the fence. She rolled a stone upon the rope of the donkey, and galloped joyfully forward to surprise her master.

Since leaving the Padre's house she had learned that a talking dog must approach people with care. Therefore Fidele gave only her familiar bark of greeting, and licked her master's hand. The sun-burned face of Salvatore creased into a smile of relief. The sheep, too, recognized her voice and became well behaved on the instant. The shepherd's first words were, "Can you talk?" "A little," said Fidele, with hesitation, showing none of the vanity that she really felt.

"Can you tell me what you want to tell me?"

"I will try, if you will give me more lessons."

The flock being sheltered for the night, the shepherd and his dog entered the cabin and kindled the fire. He sat upon his bench and

Fidele rested her chin upon his knee. "I bring you a gift," she said. "Wait."

She led the donkey right up to the supper table.

"Where did you get him?" Salvatore cried, not believing his eyes. "Always I have wanted a beautiful, strong beast like that."

"A woman gave him to me."

"Why?"

"Because I talked."

"There," Salvatore clapped his hands, "you see how right I was to have the Padre teach you. Everyone will give you presents. We shall be rich. You must go to the village and talk to the people. They will pay well."

The moon had set before the man Salvatore and his dog brought their conversation to a close. They were very happy. Each felt that a new chapter was opening in their lonely lives.

East, West, Home's Best

FOR several months after the dog had left him, the Padre was on the go, morning, noon, and night. It did not seem that there had ever been so many children, old people, and animals calling upon him to get them out of their accidents and troubles. He climbed mountains and slid down into valleys. He visited far-away farmhouses and big cities. He grew so thin that the Widow Hedge-Hog grew tired of taking tucks in the waist of his green velvet knicker-bockers to keep them from slipping down upon his red slippers. And during all these weeks there was no news of Salvatore and the conversational dog.

Late in September the Padre found himself, one afternoon, only a few miles from the cabin by the twin oaks. He had been up all the night before, getting a goat with a broken leg out of a crack in the rock, and in releasing a couple of foolish young hares from a trap. He was frightfully tired. Sure of a hearty welcome, he said to himself, "I will call on the old shepherd, and stay the night with him. I could jolly well do with a long sleep."

Approaching Salvatore's farm the Padre saw at a glance that there had been a serious change, and a change for the worse. The vegetable garden was full of weeds. The door of the chicken house had broken from its hinges and the chickens, unfed, were wandering in the woods. The dirty straw of the sheep-fold had not been shoveled out for weeks. The sheep themselves were wild and thin, and their wool was torn by thorns. Most suspicious of all, the flock was scattered over the mountain, with neither man nor dog on guard.

The well-kept cabin was also changed. Flowers no longer bloomed around the door. A pan of unwashed dishes stood on the porch. The glass of a window was broken, and a rag had been stuck into the hole.

More and more puzzled, the Padre wandered about, calling the names of Salvatore and Fidele. At last, from behind a hay-shed, he heard a groan. There, lying upon a rock, a pair of crutches beside him, his head wrapped in a soiled bandage, was the shepherd. Instantly the Padre was at his side, full of sympathy.

"My poor, brave Salvatore, what can have happened? You, who have always been so active and so healthy. Did you fall over a precipice? Were you attacked by a bull? Did a rolling rock crush you? What can be the cause of all this disorder?"

The man's eyes opened feebly. His lips moved to say two words, ". . . Talking . . . Dog . . ." and then he fainted.

The Padre did not waste a second. He realized that the man was weak from loss of blood and from lack of food. He needed a cook, a nurse and a doctor, and the Padre, by happy chance, was all three. He set milk and eggs to cook. He made the bed and put in hot stones to warm it. He managed to get the wounded man upon his back, and half-dragging, half-carrying him, brought him inside the house. He washed the cuts with hot water and salt, and re-made the bandages, wet with fresh milk.

He forced the drowsy man to swallow a little of the warm custard. Then he drove the sheep to the well, watered and fed them, talking to them all the while in their own language. The chickens he called also in their language, promising them a full meal of corn. They came, ate, and perched obediently in their house, while he propped up the broken door.

Not until Salvatore was washed and fed, his wounds more comfortable, and his mind at rest about his sheep and poultry, did the Padre return to the question which had been puzzling him ever since his arrival at the farm. "How under the sun was Fidele the cause of all this misery?"

"When she came back she was all right," said Salvatore, "but after a few days she changed. She gave me orders about the sheep. She wanted me to stay in the house and give her talking lessons. She used to run to the village, and talk all day at the cafe. They gave her white wine to drink. Everybody complimented her. She told all she knew. She said you told her to talk with many people. She talked all the time. She is a female dog. I could not stop her."

"Then she learned to sing. It was not musical singing. I drove her outdoors with a stick, and she did not come home for a week."

"She told the Calderon family that I burned the brushwood on the common fields to make the young grass stronger for my lambs. It does make the grass grow stronger. It hurt no one to burn that brush. But they threw stones at me from behind a wall. The stones cut the skin on my head. I lay like one dead for three hours.

"At the cafe they told Fidele that she could earn a beef-steak for dinner every day if she would go to the cities and speak for people in the theatres. Their talk turned her head. She wanted me to sell my sheep and go to the town with her. What a foolishness! Me, who have raised sheep for fifty years, to be a play-actor in a hall with a dog. So she ran away with a man who bought her a silver collar."

"It was a mistake, Padre, to teach her to talk. Do not think, my honored Don Porko, that I blame you. It was my fault. It was I who urged you to do it. She was the wisest sheep-guard that I ever had. How was I to know that when a good dog tries to be more than a dog, she will be worse than a bad dog?"

Caring for the animals and nursing the old shepherd back to health, the Padre remained in the cabin by the twin oaks for fifteen days. He soon had the garden in better order. He planted purple daisies about the doorstep. Being constantly together, he and Salvatore became close friends. They spoke often of Fidele, and the riddle of her flighty character. The old man's conclusion was always the same, "She had enough sense to be a dog, but not enough sense to be a man."

"No," the Padre would object kindly, "per-

haps it was not that. Perhaps it was that the
new learning came to her too quickly before
her brain was prepared to use it. It upset her
judgment. But sometime, I am sure that her
good dog-sense will return. A good dog is a
pretty fine person. It was the flattery that she
received at the village that stole away her
brains. Sometime she will wake up and try to
come back, and then she will be a better dog
than she ever was before."

To celebrate his last supper in the cabin,
the Padre was cooking his famous recipe of
sausages and beans. Salvatore was knitting, as
mountain shepherds often do to while away
the empty hours. He wanted to finish another
red sock to match the red slippers, before the
Padre's departure. Neither of them heard the
slight scratch at the door. It came again, louder.

"Somebody is on the veranda," said the
Padre, trotting across to lift the latch. The
head of a thin, tired dog looked in. All the

gloss was gone from her ruddy coat, and all the self-confidence from her manner. Her ears and tail drooped, and her paws were sore. It was Fidele, but an unbelievably altered Fidele. She was no longer the heroine of the cafe, setting out to win untold beef-steaks in the cities.

"May I come in, Salvatore?" she asked doubtfully. "I desire only to watch your sheep, and never to talk again. I ran away from that horrible man. He locked me in a box, only let-

ting me out to speak in the theatre. When he was drunk he beat me. He beat me because I made mistakes. I was so frightened that I never said the right words. I hate towns; I hate man's talk. I want to be your dog, and to lie in the sunshine guarding sheep." Hesitantly, she limped across the room, and laid her muzzle on the shepherd's knee. The knitting needles clicked on. Salvatore refused to look at her. But a battle was being fought in his heart.

The Padre gave a final professional stir to his sausages and beans. He put Fidele's bowl on the floor—princely sausage upon a throne of beans—but the dog refused to go near it until Salvatore had looked at her.

"So you don't want to talk any more?" The Padre broke a long silence. "It is well. I like dogs and I like men, but we should not mix the two. I heard your first word, and I hope that I have now heard your last word. But, you are letting my incomparable stew get cold."

It was after supper. The dog had not moved from the shepherd's knee. She was looking passionately into his eyes, whimpering and raising her paw.

"Look, she wants to tell me something," exclaimed Salvatore with interest. And then for the single time in human memory, Don Padre Porko lost his temper, and he lost it violently.

"Well, you let her keep on wanting to," he squealed, stamping all four feet at once. "You are a mutton-headed old fool, sillier than your own sheep. It is good for her to want to tell you something. Every dog wants to speak to the person he loves. That's what makes him a good dog, but if ever Fidele tries really to say it, you hit her over the head with a sharp ax. If you don't, I will. We've had enough nonsense about talking dogs. Let dogs stay dogs."

And Don Porko threw the frying-pan back on the fire, spilling two sausages and quite a few perfectly good beans.

A BULLY Learns a Lesson

ome in, come in, if you are a friend,"
invited the Padre, trying to button
his pantaloons and put on his red slippers all
at the same time. The thin neck of Professor
Stork pushed through the crack of the door.

"We are many friends. In fact, a delegation."
He stalked impressively into the room, his
black wings folded over his snow-white body,
his bill and legs nicely polished. "I may even
go so far as to describe us as a referendum of
the bipeds, the quadrupeds and the octopeds."
He nodded indulgently at the ants and beetles
who were scurrying between his toes.

"Come in, everybody, glad to see you. The
beetles and the black ants had better climb up

on the table, where they can see better," smiled the Padre hospitably. "And you, Professor Red-legs, try to forget that you are a school teacher and don't use those long words. I don't understand them."

The stork was followed by the dog, the cat, the squirrel, the rabbit, the red hen, the frog, the goat, and the donkey, who only put her head through the doorway. "I'm afraid it would be crowded if all of me came in," she brayed.

"We have elected Professor Red-legs to be the talker," croaked the frog. The stork cleared his throat, which took quite a while as it was so long, and folding one red leg inside his white vest, he began.

"We have come, Chief, to ask your permission to break the animals' law."

"You mean our law that whatever men may do to us we must forgive them, serve them willingly, and never do them harm?" asked the Padre quickly.

"That is the one," replied the Professor solemnly. "But in this case we animals have a terrible provocation. It is the butcher's boy, Ricardo . . ."

"He is cruel," barked the dog.

"He is horrid," cackled the red hen.

"He is a brute," bleated the goat.

"He is a hateful bully," mewed the cat.

The Padre put his feet over his ears, crying, "Order, order. We must get these complaints straight. Go around the circle, beginning with you, Professor, and everyone tell me what is wrong with Ricardo."

"He climbed upon the Roman ruins where my family and I spend the winter," said the stork. "It was at noon, while we were having our nap. He caught my wife and pulled the three first feathers out of her right wing. Now, when she flies she goes around in circles and that horrible boy rolls on the grass with laughter."

"He drowned my four kittens," sobbed the cat, "after the master had said that I could keep one of them as company for my old age."

"He has a sharp pin in the end of a stick, and jabs it into me to see me jump," said the donkey.

"He empties my dinner into the garbage pail before I can eat it," growled the dog.

"I had a nest of thirteen eggs, all ready to hatch, and he walked on them, on purpose," wailed the red hen.

"He kicks our houses to pieces, out of pure meanness," said the ants.

"Perhaps you are right." The Padre was thoughtful. "He will soon be a man, and if he is not cured before then, he will remain cruel all his life. But it is a serious thing to break the animals' law of willing obedience to man. When do you want to teach him his lesson?"

"On Tuesday, when he returns from the

Villatoro market," they answered promptly.

"Well, I will give you permission, because in the end it will be a kindness to Ricardo. But there must be no roughness. Nothing to really hurt him."

"Thank you, thank you, Padre," all the animals exclaimed. "Certainly, nothing to injure him. Just a gentle act of self-defense on our part."

Professor Redlegs put his

bill confidentially close to the Padre's ear. "And if you would enjoy a good laugh, Chief, be at the eucalyptus grove about two o'clock on Tuesday."

It was the day and the hour appointed. The sun beat hotly upon the dusty road. Ricardo had sold his cheeses and goose livers under the awning in the square at Villatoro, and was trotting toward the shady grove where he usually ate his lunch on market days. "Goodness, I am hungry," he said to himself, "and won't I have a long, cool drink from my bottle."

He tied the donkey, slipped off his heavy shoes and coat, and sat down with his back to a tree and the lunch-basket between his knees. In the basket was a covered dish in which his mother always put something particularly tasty on market days. "I wonder what she has given me today," he said, lifting the cover. A dead mouse and two green caterpillars lay inside. In a nearby tree a cat was holding her sides with laughter. "Ugh," Ricardo cried, disgusted. "Anyway, I'll have a good drink." But the bottle was empty; some strong teeth had worked the cork loose. "Everything goes wrong today, but at least I will have a sleep, here in the shade." As he rested, eyes closed, he did not see a stork wing slowly toward the Roman ruins, with a pair of shoes hanging from his bill, nor a dog walk carefully out of the grove with a folded coat in his mouth.

The beetles approached the boy's head and the black ants assembled at his feet. "You go in first," said the beetles, "and when you are all inside his trouser legs, two of us will go inside each ear and four of us into his nose."

Poor Ricardo leaped into the air. The whole inside of his head crawled. It was frightful. Just at that moment the black ants inside his trousers began to bite. No boy had ever been more painfully attacked.

"There are ghosts here," he shouted. "Let me get away. Let me get away. Where are my shoes? Where is my coat, with the money bag?" He ran toward his donkey, but sharp squirrels' teeth had cut the rope, and she moved briskly away, always keeping just out of Ricardo's reach. To make matters worse, those same teeth had also gnawed the strap that held the saddle in place. Now it fell to the ground, so the unfortunate boy was obliged to carry it himself.

Donkey and boy went forward for a long time, the boy limping because of the thistles and thorns in his bare feet, the donkey always just a few feet ahead, and choosing to cross the thickest hedges, the muddiest ditches, and the sharpest stones. "Oh, I shall die of thirst," groaned Ricardo, shifting the heavy saddle from one shoulder to the other. They had come to a region where he had never been before.

A welcome sound reached his ears. He stopped. It was the cool croak of a frog. "Oh," he thought, "what luck! Where there are frogs there is water." He went in the direction of the croak. Sure enough, there was a deserted well. But it was deep. He leaned far over the edge, to see whether he might not touch the water with his handkerchief. It was then that the goat, coming noiselessly from behind a bush, gave him a butt that sent him splashing into the well. The water was waist deep.

"Help, help." His cries re-echoed through the forest. Presently they took on a shrill note of fear. "O-o-o-e-e-e-eee, the well is full of snakes. I can feel them squshing between my toes. O-o-o-o-eee. Help, help!"

From the bottom of the well, Ricardo

watched the sun move slowly toward the west.
He was entirely exhausted. He had shouted for
help until he could not shout another word.
The water, which had seemed so cool at first,
now felt freezing. His stomach, that he usually
filled so generously, was terribly empty. He
wanted to die, and hoped that it would happen
quickly.

A squeaky voice spoke his name from the
top of the well, "Are you there, Ricardo?"

"Yes, here I am," he answered, his teeth
chattering. "Please, please help me out of this
awful place."

"Not so fast," squeaked the unseen visitor.
"Do you remember the animals who have
served you so well? They have guarded your
home, they have carried you about, they have
given you milk and honey and eggs. Tell me,
truthfully, how have you treated them? What
would happen to you, if they should be as cruel
to you as you have been to them?"

The cold and frightened Ricardo was thinking hard, but he was ashamed to make a reply.

"We are the Animal Kingdom, we who are
speaking to you. We will get you out of the well.
We will take you home. We will give back all
that you have lost. But only if you will give us
your solemn word, cross-your-heart, that you
will keep the golden rule toward us animals,
to do to us as you would have us do to you."

"I promise, oh, I promise," cried Ricardo,
with a sob. "Please forgive me. I did not think.
I did not mean to be horrid. I'm sorry for the
things I did."

A rope was descending into the hole. "Wrap
it around you, under your arms, and we will
pull you out. But don't forget the promise.
Next time, we will leave you to the snakes."
The squeaky voice gave a command. Ricardo
thought that he heard a scraping of hoofs, a
flapping of wings, a scratching of paws. The
rope tightened, and up he came from the well.

But when he climbed over the edge, not a living thing was to be seen of his late rescuers.

Nearby was his donkey, patiently waiting to be saddled. There were his shoes, and his coat, with the money in the pocket. And there was a basket of cherries, which seemed to be a present. His stick was there too, but the pin was gone from the end.

Except the donkey, not a living thing was in sight. And yet, Ricardo thought that he saw something queer disappearing among the trees. It seemed to be a short person, with a long pink nose, wearing green knickerbockers with gold buttons. But of course that could never have been true.

The Money-Bag of
NEIGHBOR FELIX

*F*or persons who are large about the waist, and who enjoy big dinners, a cup of hot mint tea is an excellent drink. Upon a summer afternoon the Padre was making his annual trip to the mint patch, gathering his winter's supply of the sweet-smelling herb. He would bite off the stems just above the roots and lay them evenly in baskets. The Widow Hedge-Hog would later dry them in the sun, and tie them in bundles to a nail in the kitchen ceiling, until they were needed for the tea-pot.

Already the pile of green foliage nearly touched the rim of his basket. Suddenly his quick ears pricked up; somebody was coming. It was a cane, tap-tap-tapping upon a gravel path. He raised his head, to peek through the underbrush. Lame Felix, who lived near the eucalyptus hedge, was coming, but he was acting in a very strange way. He would walk a few steps, and stop, and wave his stick, as though attacking some enemy. And, although he was alone, he was talking a perfect stream. Queerest of all, he was crying real tears, a thing that grown-up men almost never do.

The Padre wiped the loose mint leaves from the corners of his mouth and stepped toward the patch. "Good afternoon, Neighbor Felix. You do not seem very happy. Is something the matter?"

The lame man scowled. "The pirates," he burst out, ferociously. "The brigands. The black-hearted robbers. I have been to the police station to make a complaint, but all that donkey of an Aurelio can say is, 'We shall see what we shall see.' But will that get me back my bag of pesetas?"

"Well, Neighbor Felix, come help me gather a few more mint plants. Then we will fix up your trouble, whatever it may be."

Felix stared. "You think that you can, Don Porko?"

"Why of course we can. Haven't you always been kind to us animals? We animals can do anything that we really want."

The two of them worked for a while without speaking. "Now come along home with me, and let's hear the whole story," said the Padre briskly.

A little later Felix was seated in the rocking chair, his mouth full of peach jam. "Pretty tasty, isn't it?" asked the Padre, licking the last drop from the spoon. "The peaches were a present from the General's orchard. The rabbit family brought me nearly a bushel. Just for teaching them how to throw the hunting dogs off their track. Simplest thing in the world— winding wild cabbage leaves around their feet.

But what was it, Felix, that you went to the police station about?"

At once Felix's anger burned anew. "They wore new coats, they were polite, those two robbers. I would never have trusted them, except that they know my nephew, Luque, who keeps a store in the town. They had heard from him of the bitter spring, and they came to buy that worthless corner of my land. Nothing will grow there. Neither people nor animals can drink the water—it tastes like medicine. When they offered me five hundred silver pesetas for it, it seemed a gift straight from the saints in heaven.

"That was yesterday morning. We drove sticks into the ground to mark how much they had bought. They paid me the money and I took it home. In the afternoon we went to the lawyer's and signed the paper. But when I returned last night, and put my hand behind the loose brick in the chimney, the money was not there. Not only the new money was gone, but the old money also, the coins I have been saving all my life, to buy food when I cannot work."

Felix's tears began afresh. "I understand how they did it. It was the tall one who paid me, and who went with me to the lawyer's. During that time the short one had hidden himself inside my house, to learn where I keep my money. But I'll catch them yet, the deceitful, lying robbers of the poor!"

The Padre listened with close attention. "Does anyone know where you keep your money?" he questioned.

"Not a soul on earth, since my good wife died twelve years ago."

"Did you tell anyone that you had sold the bitter spring for five hundred pesetas?"

"Not a soul, not a . . . that is to say, no one except my cousin Moreno, who pastures his sheep in my field. It was such a huge piece of luck that I was bursting to tell someone, and I told him, as I was fetching the money home yesterday at noon."

"And of course Moreno knows that you keep your money in the house?" continued the Padre. "In the chimney, or under your bed, or inside the woodpile. He knows about that, doesn't he?"

"Where else would a man hide his money?" said Felix, innocently.

The Padre's expression was serious. "I want you to promise me one thing, Neighbor Felix. If I get your bag of pesetas back, you must take it, quick, to the bank in the village. They can take better care of it than you can. Do you promise?"

"Yes, ten times, yes," said the lame man, holding up his right hand. "I promise. If I ever get it back, that is," he concluded mournfully.

"Your cousin Moreno lives in that stone

cottage near the top of the hill, doesn't he?"

"Yes, but don't you go near it, Don Padre. He has two of the worst dogs in Spain. They would enjoy tearing you into little bits."

The Padre shook hands with the old canal worker, slipping a jar of the peach jam into his pocket as a present. "What I want of you, Felix, is to go straight home. Do not say a word to anyone. I'll call on you early tomorrow morning. I have a feeling that you will see your money again, if your animal friends are as clever as I think they are."

As Felix and his cane stumped away, the Padre went to his kitchen pantry, pulled open the drawer where Mrs. Hedge-Hog kept the cheese and whispered, "Are you there, Scratchy?" Within the wall was a faint movement, and presently, popping up from nowhere, a sleek gray mouse was perched on the tea-pot.

"Did you call me, Chief?" he asked, smoothing his whiskers. "I was taking a short rest."

"I want you to do some detective work for me tonight, Scratchy, the kind that you do so beautifully. Get your supper early, and have some more sleep. I'll call again in two hours."

As twilight descended, the Padre, with his velvet jacket buttoned under his chins, and with Scratchy reposing in his pocket, was climbing the path to the house of Moreno, the shepherd.

Two white Pyrenean dogs, showing their teeth, came bounding to meet him. When they saw who it was their tails wagged and they whined a welcome. "I have a little friend," said

the Padre, "whom I want to leave in the shepherd's kitchen until the moon sets. I will be back about four o'clock and I don't want you fellows to kick up a row. Is Moreno in the house?"

"No, he is closing the sheep in the barn," said the dogs.

"Good." The Padre was explaining to Scratchy what his detective duties were to be. "Go through that crack under the door and hide somewhere. Try to see everything that the man does. If he goes into the woodshed, follow him. You must manage to see everything. I will be back for you just before sunrise, and will scrape my foot on the doorstep. We are counting on you, Scratchy." Like a puff of dust the gray mouse was out of sight. And with a goodnight to the dogs and compliments upon the fine coats they were putting on for the winter, the Padre retraced his path.

When his plans were working smoothly, it was the Padre's pleasant custom to compose songs as he walked along. His legs would beat time to the tune— one, two, one, two. Also he loved to sing, and to make up rhymes about vegetables and puddings. As he trotted downhill from Moreno's, with the

stars bright overhead, he felt at peace with all the world and wanted to sing.

Oh Heaven is a garden
Where Easter flowers grow,
The Angels are the gardeners
Each with a rake and hoe,
The strawberries, big as apples,
Hang heavy on the trees,
And the perfume of the onion
Floats gently on the breeze.

The Padre hummed it over again but it didn't seem a very good song. Something was left out. True poetry was not in it. It left a singer feeling empty. But a big thought was being born. The Padre sat upon the root of a tree and shut his eyes, so as not to miss it. Pig-gish poets and poetical pigs, all, all artists must know disappointment. If his song had missed fire, he would re-compose it. And soon his care-free tenor squeal was winging sentimentally down the hillside, flinging aloft another set of words.

The pearls of Heaven are turnips,
    The ruby beets are fine,
The emeralds are spinach,
    And lettuce in a line,
The saints who rake the garden,
    Have a single, lovely dream,
To stew their golden carrots
    In butter and in cream.

Ah, that was something like. Here was real poetry, particularly the ending. He took a deep breath and sang it again, putting some extra curlicues in the tune.

    . . . . . a single, lovely dream-m-m-m
    Stewed in butter and in cream-m-m-m-m.

"It is certainly one of the best little things that I've dashed off in some time," he said, opening his own gate. But Mrs. Hedge-Hog was indignant. Here he was, late for supper again. And all that row! Did he think that he was a drunken canary, caroling on the public streets? He made her catarrh worse, she said, and rolled herself up into a ball.

The greater part of the night the Padre dozed in his arm-chair, but before sunrise was back upon the shepherd's porch, giving the signal. The shaggy dogs had pretended not to see him. Scratchy scrambled into his pocket, but not a word was uttered until they were back in the Padre's pantry and the latter had found a slice of cheese for the detective. "You must be faint, my dear fellow. Take a hearty nibble or two, and then tell me every single thing that Moreno did." Scratchy cleaned his mustache with a gentlemanly swish, and sat up.

"The shepherd first put the bar on the door and the shutter on the window. He built a big fire and heated his bean soup. It tasted real good. I had some later on, when he was in bed. Two or three times he opened the door to make sure that the dogs were on guard. Finally he went to a pile of wood in the corner, reached under it and took out a sack. It seemed heavy. From the inside of the chimney he brought out a smaller sack. Saying something about it all being his now, he emptied the money of the smaller sack into the big one. He took the big sack to the back room. I stood in the doorway and watched. He tried several places, but at last put it behind a loose board that is above the middle of the window. He seemed very satisfied and rubbed his hands together. Then he slept and didn't move again."

"You are a born detective, Scratchy," said the Padre. "And I think that you have helped a poor old man out of his trouble. Take a few more crumbs of cheese and have a good sleep. I'll have a nap myself, and a hot shower, and then go over to Felix's."

The genial Padre's mind was distressed. Would it ever be possible, he wondered, to teach men to be as honest to one another as their animals were? Why must men and women be spiteful, selfish and unfair? But a good breakfast made him more optimistic, and his smile was as bright as the new day when he entered Felix's bean patch.

"I didn't sleep a wink," scolded Felix. "Have you found those burglars yet?"

"Come and take a walk," suggested the Padre, soothingly. "Let's follow the canal and see your bitter spring."

Felix went over and over the story of his robbery in a very tiresome way. He and the Padre had come quite a distance when the latter asked, "Is that the spring, down there, where the two men are digging?"

The lame man jumped into the air. "What two men? Where? Yes, yes, come quick; they are the thieves themselves." Shaking his cane, he ran toward the spring.

"You burglars, you criminals. Where is my money? Give it back or I'll have you in prison."

The men, up to their knees in smelly mud, looked at one another in astonishment. "Your money, Senor Felix? We have seen no money, since we paid you for this land, two days ago."

Old Felix was truly a pitiable sight. The savings of his lifetime were gone. He saw no future but to starve.

"But why did you buy this bitter spring?" he persisted. "Why are you digging it out? Nothing grows here."

"This water we have taken to the doctors," said the tall man. "They say that it will make sick people well. We believe that we can sell the water of this spring as medicine. But as for stealing your pesetas, Senor Felix, that idea never came into our minds, we assure you."

"I'll tell you what to do." The Padre patted his shoulder comfortingly. "You go for a long walk. Find your cousin Moreno, ask his advice, walk together to the police station, and perhaps the fat Aurelio will have discovered something. Then invite Moreno to dinner at your house. Something may turn up. You never can tell. And, above all, remember your promise—to take the sack of money straight to the bank if ever you get your hand on it again."

Felix and Moreno obeyed the Padre's advice. From the police office they returned to Felix's cabin to cook their meal. A white towel lay on the table. Felix snatched it off. Behold, safe and sound, in the middle of the table was the missing bag of pesetas. Felix hugged it. He kissed it. He laughed and he cried, both at the same time.

"Where did it come from? How did it get here? It is a miracle. I don't understand it at all." Then he gave himself the keen pleasure

of counting the coins. His excited joy was re-
doubled. For there were ninety extra pesetas
in the bag. He did not try to check the torrent
of his jubilant speech. "Do you understand it,
Moreno?" he kept asking. "All my own is back,
and more too."

Moreno gazed uneasily out the door and up
to his own house. The savage dogs were keeping guard. But he thought it safer not to say a
word. There was a great deal in this that he
could not understand. For one thing, that white
towel on the table came from his house. For
another, his own savings had been ninety pesetas. He'd do well to keep very quiet.

As Felix was taking his hat and stick to go to
the bank, a new thought bubbled up in his
brain. "It might have been that Padre Porko
who stole the money? He's a pretty sharp fellow. He knows everything. And he put in the
extra pesetas because his conscience hurt him.
It must be that."

"He might well have been the dishonest one," Moreno answered.

PABLO'S GOOSE

and the Evil Eye

*A*s Pablo, who was about nine years old, came out of school one day, a crowd of people were reading a notice on the wall of the Mayor's Office. Being small and skinny, Pablo easily crawled between their legs. The notice said that the Governor of Gu-ad-al-a-jara, determined to defend the honor of his beloved geese, would give a prize of one hundred silver pesetas for the finest goose that should be hatched and reared that season in his province. The geese would be judged the week before Christmas, and the fortunate goose would be sent, a ribbon round his neck, to the King for his New Year's Dinner. More than that, the person who raised the goose would receive a medal, marked, "My Geese are Fit for the King."

As he read the notice, skinny little Pablo felt himself swelling. Was not that the very day that his own goose was due to hatch her ten eggs? He ran all the way home. He approached the box under the fig tree where his goose was setting, and reached under her. Three of the eggs were cracking. And the next day, when he raced home from school, his old goose was strutting about with six fuzzy goslings behind her. Then came accidents. One would much rather skip them, but they happened. An alley cat ate one of the goslings. A mule stepped on one. Two others, over-adventurous, swam out too far upon the village pond and were pulled under by the fierce water rats. At the end of two months, one child alone remained to Pablo's mother goose.

But what a gosling he was! As though Nature were trying to make up for the brothers and sisters who had been killed, he was a miracle goose. He was strong and white. His beak and legs were a bright orange. He could swim as fast as his mother. And eat? Why, he ate more, and ate faster, and ate longer than any gosling in the village. Pablo could almost see him grow.

In the morning when the boy opened the door of the shed, the King's Goose—for already they had nicknamed him that—would be the first out, and the first at the water's edge for his drink and bath. Then he would be at the pasture long before the others, pecking the grass while the dew still glistened upon it. During the mid-day heat, while the rest of the geese enjoyed a nap, he was back at his work, taking nourishment.

People soon remarked Pablo's goose. Never had they seen such a one! He wanted to grow. His one thought was to stuff himself with food, to grow big, and bigger. Here was something new to talk about, the goose-girls realized. And they did talk, freely. The peddlers who drive their carts among the farmhouses of Gu-ad-al-a-jara, selling earthen pots and soup kettles, and canvas sandals, and dried fruit, and pinafores, and needles and thread, all saw Pablo's goose, and spread the story. It was the sort of news that everyone was pleased to repeat. The goose that would win the Governor's prize had already been found, they said.

Walking to and from school, Pablo's mind buzzed with plans as to how he would spend the hundred silver pesetas. First of all, he would buy a new black shawl with a silk fringe for his mother. Then a pair of spectacles for his grandmother. A box of tobacco for his father. A knife with a big and a little blade for himself. And with the money that might be left, a pudding full of raisins and candied figs, and so big that all the relations and neighbors might each have a slice.

The days flowed uneventfully into one another. For the King's Goose, life was an unbroken carnival of eating, swimming, and of waiting for daylight, so that he might start eating again. Each day brought nearer the exciting event of choosing the King's New Year's dinner. Midsummer turned into September and barely four months remained until the prize winner should be named.

And then, without warning, something went terribly wrong. Arriving home from school, the boy found his goose wandering up and down, not even trying to eat. He held his head in a crooked way. Nor would he drink or swim.

"Don't you worry about him," said his mother encouragingly. "He'll be all right in the morning. Probably he's eaten a snake or a lizard which hasn't digested well."

But all the next day, still holding his head in that awkward position, the King's Goose followed the others, not swallowing anything. This state of things continued for a week. The goose grew thinner and thinner. He sat all day in a corner of the yard, eyes shut and his wings drooping. Pablo was entirely disconsolate. He brought the veteran goose-growers of the whole province to see the sick creature, but none of them could offer any real help. And when Pablo picked up his goose to carry him into the warm kitchen at night he was shocked to find him hardly heavier than a skeleton.

Great-Aunt Teresa finally gave the explanation which was generally accepted. Someone had put the Evil Eye on the King's Goose. Some bad-hearted or ill-natured person, who was in league with the Devil, had put a curse upon him. But who would have been mean enough to do this to Pablo? Everyone liked both the boy and his family. The whole village was proud of the fabulous young bird. And most of them were secretly counting upon having a slice of the pudding, once the prize was won.

Whenever the boy was not at school, or helping his father in the grain fields, he sat mournfully beside his goose, aching to be able to help him. He arranged a basket of hay for him in the kitchen, beside the chimney. In the evening he would often fall asleep on the floor beside the basket. And all the time he was wishing, wishing, with might and main, for some cure, some medicine.

There came a night when the goose seemed to be dying. For two days he had not moved his head from under his wing. When all the household was asleep, Pablo slipped out of bed, lighted his candle at the fireplace and lay on the

floor beside the dull creature that had so re-
cently been the active and beautiful King's
Goose. He wished and wished, and wished, that
he could help, or that he knew someone who
might help.

Pablo has never been sure just when the
shadowy visitor came into the kitchen. No door
opened or shut. The candle gave so dim a light
that the boy did not see distinctly. The visitor
had a pink round face, and moved silently and
deftly. He lifted the head of the dying goose
and listened to its breathing. Then he stood in
the doorway and spoke to the bats who were
darting among the fruit trees catching moths.
He gave his orders like the captain of a ship.

"Fly to the Roman ruin, you bats. Don't
waste a second. Tell the stork to come here.
Tell him that the Padre Porko orders him to
come, in a case of life or death. If he says that he
cannot find the place, you stay and guide him to
this door. Quick, fly."

Pablo lived to be a very old man, but he was now treated to the most astonishing spectacle of his whole life. A pig with bright eyes, and as nimble on his feet as a kitten, wearing a red beret and green velvet trousers, brought the candle and set it upon an upturned pail near the goose's basket. Beside him stood a sober, black and white bird, with long legs, and a sharp thin bill. The figure in the red beret held the goose's open mouth towards the candle, and the stork put its thin bill far down inside the throat of the goose.

"Feel all around, Professor. Explore everywhere. There is surely something. But be gentle and don't push it down his windpipe," said the Padre.

The stork drew out his bill and nodded. "Yes, it's there, as you thought it would be. It seems to be a splinter of wood, split like a triangle. It lies across the opening where he swallows. The ends are caught in the soft flesh.

Hold him tight, Chief, and I'll try to pull it out in one piece."

The goose felt the scraping inside his throat; he half opened his eyes. When he saw the forked twig that the stork withdrew in his beak, he swallowed twice. He drew in his wings and tried to stand, but was too weak.

"Excuse me, Professor, for leaving you without ceremony, but I must get him some strengthening food," said the Padre. "He has nearly starved to death. Sorry to have broken into your sleep, but thank you for coming. It was worth doing, wasn't it? He is a fine animal, and the boy is good to our people, too."

With a basket in his mouth, the Padre was already trotting out of the yard. Where the river widens, the current is sluggish, and a tiny white blossom grows upon the surface of the water. Leaning out from the bank, the Padre scooped a number of these floating plants into his basket and hurried back to Pablo's. He

rummaged among the supplies of Pablo's
mother, and found corn meal and salt. Tearing
the flowers into fine pieces, he made a dough of
them and the corn meal, with a pinch of salt.
He rolled the dough into balls, about as big as
cherries. "Now, my friend," he said to the
King's Goose, "I mustn't give you too much
all at once. I'll give you ten pills now, and each
half hour you are to take ten more. The white
flower is just the tonic you need.

"But I ought to scold you a little, King's
Goose," continued the Padre. "You nearly
starved because of this twig in your throat, and
it was your own fault. You are too greedy. You
try to eat all the food there is, before the others
get to the table. You are so anxious to eat that
you do not examine what you eat. If you want
to grow up and be a credit to your mother, and
to Pablo, and win the Governor's prize, take
smaller mouthfuls, and swallow them slower."

Then the visitor turned to Pablo. "You saw

what I gave him, the white flower pills. For a week give him all he will eat—here in the yard, before you let him go back to the goose pasture."

The King's Goose had lifted his head, the good old ravenous look in his eye. The corn meal pills were disappearing as by magic. Pablo got up to say his thanks properly, but no one was there. He and his goose were alone. "But there was a person here—I know there was, I saw him," he cried, picking up the candlestick and running to the door. He saw nothing but a glimmer, which might have been the reflection of candlelight on a vanishing gold button.

The WHITE SISTER

The Padre had been out since midnight, nursing an old wood-chopper whose ax had slipped and cut his foot. Taking a short cut through the woods he came face to face with a sight that took his breath away. Three little girls were seated upon a rock. Their eyes were big and sleepy. To be warmer they were leaning against one another, and the oldest had tucked her shawl around the knees of them all. The Padre stopped, rubbing his eyes to make sure that he was awake.

"Bless my starry garters!" he exclaimed. "Do you young ladies live here all the time? I know a good many people, but I don't think that we have met before."

"Oh, no," said the biggest girl, who sat in the middle, an arm around the smaller sister on either side. "We are waiting for the White Sister."

The Padre wrinkled his forehead. "I'm afraid that I don't know her either. But she sounds nice."

The little girls made room for him on their rock, and he sat down beside the littlest one, who gave him the fringe of the shawl to cover his feet. A bit from one, and a bit from another, he heard their whole story. Their father was a soldier at the war. A beggar woman had brought a piece of paper saying that he was a prisoner in a camp, inside a high fence of wire. Their mother had gone to try to find him. And every evening a strange, quiet visitor, dressed in a white wool cloak and hood, and wearing a wooden cross over her heart, had come to care for them.

"She comes like a cloud, without any sound,"

exclaimed the littlest one. "Her feet hardly touch the ground. And she brushes our hair until it shines and does it in braids before she puts us to bed."

"Her hands are cool and soft," said the middle-sized girl. "Like a cool wind on a hot day. She never scolds."

The eldest girl, evidently feeling her responsibility, was practical. "She brought us bread. And always with something else. Once it was cheese, and once honey. And once some eggs. She gave us some soap that smelled like flowers, and a candle so that we should not be afraid when there were noises."

"But there are men who do not like her because of her wooden cross," broke in the littlest one. "They hid in the bushes to catch her. When they knocked on our door we did not pull the bolt until the White Sister was out of the pantry window. After that she told us to meet her by this rock. But tonight she has not come."

"That sounds serious," said the Padre, scratching his ear as he thought very hard. "Tell me, did you ever notice her shoes? Whether there was earth or dust on the toes? Think before you answer. On her toes, was there black earth, or red earth, or white dust?"

"It was white dust, all over her shoes," replied the middle girl. "And white dust on the bottom of her cloak."

"Then she must have come from the hills, to the north of us, where the forest and the rocks are," said the Padre. "It is there that we must search first.

"And what have you young ladies had for your supper?" he continued, laying his paw on his own empty stomach, for he was terribly hungry.

The smaller girls looked up at their elder sister. "We only ate when she came the last time," she said.

The Padre jumped to his feet. "Do you mean

to say that you had no supper last night, and no dinner yesterday either? What a stupid I am, to keep you talking like this, when you must be nearly starved." He held out his two front feet. "You come straight home with me. You two little ones each take one of my hands and you, big sister, catch hold of my tail. Like that no one will stray from the path. It will soon be daylight. My house is just behind that hill." He was laughing to himself as they walked along. "In all my life," he chuckled, "this is the first time my tail was of any use. Do you like carrots? There is honey at my house, too."

The Padre walked slowly so that no one should trip over the roots. Soon they were in his sitting room and he was on his knees, blowing the fire under the covered saucepan that the Widow Hedge-Hog had left.

"You cut the bread, big sister," he called, between puffs. "And you, middle sister, get four bowls and four spoons in the pantry and set the table. And you, littlest one, stir that jar of honey, round and round, until it is soft like bean soup."

It was a grand meal and it was only after the littlest sister had fallen asleep twice, with her spoon in her mouth, that the Padre pulled down the covers of his bed. "Now you fix yourselves the best you can for the night and crawl in here for a good long nap. I'll take a walk outside and then get to sleep in my easy chair. It's five o'clock and you ought to sleep until noon."

With a saucer in his hand he went into the garden. The sky was as blue as newly-washed bluebells, with lines of pink and yellow in the place where the sun would soon come marching into sight.

"I'd better talk this over with the bees, right away," he said to himself. "Some of them may be astir already."

At the further end of his garden were six boxes, each with a cornucopia roof of straw, in which his bees had their home. The Padre set the saucer of sugar and water in the middle of the path, and peered into the little round doors of the hives. A few of the early risers had come out to observe the weather, and were combing their wings on the front piazzas.

"Come over here, my little friends," the Padre buzzed through his nose, "and get a free breakfast, while I talk to you." About a hundred worker bees flew to the dish of sweet water. "This morning I want you to do me a great favor. Never mind about gathering honey today. I want you to find a lady all in white clothes. They are white and woolly, like the back of a sheep. She is all white, white on her head and white all the way down to her feet.

Do you understand? White is the color of plum and berry flowers. She is somewhere up toward the hills, where the caves and shadowy valleys are. I want you to fly as far as you can, and to look into every dark window, into houses and barns. Look everywhere. And when you see a lady all in white, notice carefully where it is, and fly back to me here.

"Now, go into your hives and wake everybody up. Tell them the news. The Padre wants all of his bees to search for a white lady. There will be sweet water here all day, for you to drink when you return. Look into every corner. All people love the bees. You can go everywhere and be welcome."

There was a great buzz-buzz-buzzing in the six boxes and when he had seen the workers begin to fly away, by hundreds and by thousands, the Padre returned to his house, stretched out in his cushioned chair, and was soon snoring peacefully. Nor did he wake until

Mrs. Hedge-Hog, surprised at seeing three curly heads on the pillow, dropped a plate in clearing off the table.

"Excuse me," she apologized, "but the house is full of bees. The window is covered with them. They have bitten me twice on the nose. Will you kindly order them to go outside where they belong."

"Never you mind about them, my dear Widow." The Padre was hardly awake and kept getting the wrong foot into the wrong slipper. "I know what they want. Just fill our biggest pitcher with sugar and water, will you please, and take it, with six soup plates, to the garden as quickly as you can."

He was soon listening to the discoveries of his scouts. A number of them reported seeing small women, all in white and fast asleep, being rocked in boxes by old women in black.

"But those must be babies," he said with a laugh. "I'm not looking for a baby."

Other bees told of a line of figures in white, with veils over their heads, walking in a procession to a church.

"Yes, you are right," agreed the Padre, still smiling, "but those are little girls going to their confirmation. No, it is a single person, a full-sized woman, in a white wool cloak, that we must find."

Still others of his scouts told of a lady in white, holding to the arm of a man in a black coat, and followed by many young people, coming out of a mayor's office.

"Pooh," said the Padre, "that was a wedding. The woman we are looking for is probably injured, lying in some ravine, or shut inside a building."

It was well past the regular time for lunch when a very tired and bedraggled bee crept over the edge of a soup plate and took a long drink. Then it waved its front feet to attract the Padre's attention.

"Never before have I flown so far," began the bee. "I crossed two valleys to a place where the river falls down with a big noise. Inside a stone house is a woman in white. There are four towers and she is in the one over a field of clover. She sits on her bed and does not move. Her face is as white as her cloak. Outside the stone house men march up and down and there is music. But inside the window with the bars the woman does not even lift her head."

"Ah, that is the news I've been waiting for," shouted the Padre. "A stone house, you say, across two valleys, to where the water falls, and she is in the tower by the clover. Excellent, excellent. Is her window high above the ground?"

"Only about as high as a peach tree."

"And just one last question, Friend Bee, before you drink your fill of sweet water and take your rest. Did you notice any oxen, or horses, or mules, near the castle where the white lady sits?"

The bee answered between swallows. "Yes,"
—sip-sip-sip—"a herd of cows,"—sip-sip-sip—
"led by a proud young bull,"—sip-sip-sip—"in
the pasture below the tower." But the bee was
already sound asleep.

The Padre began preparations for a journey.
First he told the Widow Hedge-Hog to heat
water for the three little girls' baths. And to
give them each a cake of the pink soap that
smelled of roses. Then he got out his map to
find where, across two valleys, the river leaps
with a loud noise. And at last, having given
everybody a good bear-hug, and having re-filled
the bees' plates, and having emptied the salt
dish into his pocket, he hung a coil of light rope
around his neck and trotted away. As he disappeared in the distance Madame Hedge-Hog
heard him making up a new song, so she knew
that everything was going to turn out well. Also
she decided to cook twice as much vegetable
soup as usual.

The Proud Young Bull

THE twilight was almost gone when the Padre, lying on his stomach in the field of clover, peered up at the barred window. No soldiers were in sight. He made his voice sound like the blowing of the wind.

"Are you there, White Sister? If you are, please come to the window. I have come to take you back to the three little girls."

A shadow moved behind the bars. The face was as colorless as the hood that enshrouded it. Only the black fire of her eyes made a mark in the pale outline.

"Excuse me for breaking in upon your thoughts," he began politely, "and excuse me for not making the bow that I should. But I do not want the guards to notice me. I come from your little friends, who miss you badly, and have asked me to bring you back to them. Have you, by any chance, a spool of strong thread, or a ball of string in your pocket?"

The figure shook its head.

"Pardon me for mentioning it," he blushed a little, "but do you wear woolen stockings, and could you unravel the yarn and let one end down to me?"

The pale face smiled, showing teeth that

were whiter than her cloak, and nodded "yes."

"Then if you will kindly get it ready, I will come back when the moon rises. If you can sleep and eat before then, so much the better, as we have a long walk before us. And if the guards come to your room tell them that you will need nothing more for tonight, so that they may not come spying about your door later on."

The Padre took the risk of waving his red beret as he rolled away in the clover.

The proud three-year-old bull had eaten his fill of grass, had superintended the lying down of his family, and was having a look at the weather before settling for the night. A persuasive, thin voice interrupted the evening silence. It seemed to come from between the bars of the pasture gate.

"How wonderful it must be, to be as strong, as beautiful, as graceful, as Senor Bull."

The proud young bull snorted. "Are you talking about me, whoever you are, outside

there? You'd better be careful. I allow no liber-
ties. But speaking of strength, yes, I am strong.
Probably the strongest animal in Spain."

"I cannot help thinking," continued the persuasive tones beyond the gate, "what a pity it
is that you do nothing useful with all your
strength."

With a rumble of anger and a wicked look in
his eye, the proud young bull thrust his head
over the gate. "Now then, who are you, that
dares to come here, in my own pasture, and in-
sult me like that, you pink-nosed, flop-eared,
little bundle of impertinence?" As the bull
leaned down, the sharp points of his horns were
but a few inches from the Padre's face.

"People call me the Padre Porko."

Upon hearing these words the proud young
bull became another creature with a sudden-
ness that was laughable. "Oh, I beg your
pardon. I had no idea it was you. The light is
not good, is it? I've heard about you since I was

three days old, and I've wondered whether we should ever meet. My grandmother said she owed her life to you, that time when you lifted the fallen tree off her back. This heroic work, ahem, for me, that you spoke of, is it another of your famous kind deeds? Just call me Caesar, if you feel that you can. And tell me in plain words what you want me to do. I'm strong, but not very bright."

So the Padre brought a handful of salt out of his green velvet pocket and laid it on a flat stone, and the proud young bull licked it up with relish as the Padre explained about the three little girls and the White Lady inside the castle window.

"What we need is a plow chain," said the Padre, finishing up his explanation. "The kind that two yokes of oxen use to draw the plow, with hooks in the ends. Do you know where they are kept on your farm?"

Caesar blew through his nose, in what he intended for a smile. "We must hurry to get there and back before the moon rises. I'll show you the shed where the plows are kept. Just jump on my back, to save time. Perhaps you'd better hold on to my horns to keep from being jiggled off."

On returning to the tower above the clover field, they could see an indistinct form leaning against the bars of the window. "The guards have gone away," she whispered, "and I have let down the end of my yarn."

The Padre made the little bow with which he always saluted ladies. "I am tying my rope to the end of your yarn. Please pull it up. And to the rope I am attaching a chain with a hook on the end. Will you kindly put the hook around the middle bar of your window. It looks rusty and a little loose. Then will you please hold the hook about halfway up on the bar. Like that it will be easier for Caesar to bend. Don't be afraid, we are here to help you escape.

Caesar is frightfully strong, and I am intelligent."

The White Sister did as he directed and in the meantime the Padre had fastened the other end of the chain around the horns of the proud young bull.

Caesar braced his four feet in the soft ground of the clover field. The huge muscles of his neck and shoulders swelled out. And how he did pull! He felt that the good reputation of his grandmother and of all his family depended upon that pull. The Padre whispered admiring words in his ear. And bit by bit the rusty bar of the window bent sideways into a curve.

"That is just exactly right, my strong young friend," said the Padre, with a contented grin. "Now can you do the same thing, in the opposite direction, with the next bar?" Caesar took a deep breath and again braced his feet, while the White Sister held the hook on the bar.

After the second bar had been curved, there

was a round opening through which the White Lady could pass her head and shoulders.

"Do you think that you can come down the chain?" he asked, "very slowly, so as not to hurt yourself? We must lose no time, because I hear soldiers coming. It is not very far." The Padre was trying to look every way at once. "Please hurry all you can."

The lady was soon beside them. But the noise of the chain had been heard inside the castle, and men were looking over the wall.

"Listen to me, Caesar," said the Padre anxiously. "The White Lady and I will run to the bridge to try to cross before the guards get there. But I want you to wake your wives, and have them stand, in a crowd, close together, to bar the road, and delay the men who will follow us."

"Right you are, Chief," said the proud young bull, galloping off.

But as the Padre and the White Lady neared

the bridge they saw that other guards, with lanterns, had come out of a lower gate of the castle and were going to prevent their passage of the river.

"Oh, what shall we do?" cried the White Sister. "We are caught between the two companies of soldiers. They will surely catch us."

Behind them the Padre could hear men swearing at the herd of cows that had blocked the narrow road. In front of them the guards on the bridge were shouting to know what all the hullabaloo was about.

Breathing heavily, his hoofs clattering upon the stones, Caesar came rushing down the incline. "Jump on my back, Padre, both of you. Sit up on my neck, so you can hold my horns. I'm going to charge across the bridge. It is our only chance to get the White Sister out of here. They will be so surprised that they will not shoot."

Then occurred one of the most hair-raising

moments of the Padre's whole life. With a tri-
umphant bellow the proud young bull raced
toward the men who held the lanterns. He was
a terrifying sight. To stand in his path meant
death—and the guards promptly retreated
against the railing of the bridge.

The story of Caesar's wild dash across the
river has been recounted many times, by many
story-tellers. The proud young bull never tired
of relating it to the calves and cows of his
family, saying that it proved that if a young person is bold he will nearly always win his way.
The White Sister told it often to the three little
girls and to other young friends, who shivered
deliciously at the dangerous parts. But it was
the soldiers on the bridge who had the most
exciting tale. For they said that the bull was
no ordinary beast, but a fierce, evil spirit from
the center of the earth. They said that fire
spouted from his nostrils, and that he was rid-
den by a witch, enveloped in a white mist.

But the matter upon which every soldier dis-
agreed was the other thing on the bull's back.
A cloud came across the moon just then, and
they could not see. Some said the witch was
hump-backed, and some that she carried a sack
of bones. But no one ever guessed that the
round and bouncy object that clung to her
shoulders, as tenaciously as she clung to the
horns of the bull, was none other than that
caballero of old Spain, whose whimsical kindness is recounted in every nursery, farmhouse
kitchen, and inn parlor of all Iberia—the great
and only Senor Don Padre Porko.

Once across the bridge, the proud young bull
carried his two passengers, at a comfortable
trot, across two valleys and to the very gate of
the Padre's garden. As they jogged along they
laughed and laughed at the scare they had given
the soldiers.

"I tell you what I'm going to do," said the
proud young bull, his laugh rumbling all the

way up from his hoofs. "The men will surely be guarding the bridge to prevent my return. Therefore I will swim the stream, down below the falls, where it is shallow. As they don't see me come back they will believe, without question, that I am a bull of the Devil. I do hope that we may all meet again soon, for I've never had so much fun before."

So they all shook hands, as the Padre opened the gate, and Caesar's goodby was so loud that it made the windows rattle. They found the three little girls sitting up in bed, trying to decide whether the noise was thunder.

The White Sister leaned over them, tears of joy in her eyes, and the four hugged one another to their hearts' content.

"Now," said the White Sister, throwing back her hood, and bringing a brush out of an inside pocket of her cloak, "I'm going to brush your hair until it shines, and then put it in pig-tails —oh, excuse me"—she glanced at the Padre—

"in braids, I meant to say, for the night. Every lady should have shining hair, and I mean my three adopted children to be real ladies."

The White Sister sat on the edge of the bed, and the littlest girl bent her head forward, obediently. "I want you to start at the beginning," said the Sister, "when you went to the wood to meet me. Tell every single thing that has happened since then. Afterward I will tell how the soldiers caught me and put me in the tower of the castle."

While these domestic matters were going forward, the Padre felt that he was not needed. He lighted his pipe and strolled outside. A woman was hurrying up the path from the village.

"I live in the second cottage after the flour-mill," she said. "I would never disturb the Padre Porko so late at night, only I am in deep trouble. My three little girls are lost. Since this morning I have been looking for them. There is no sign of them in our house and the neigh-

bors have not seen them since yesterday. For a
week I have been away to visit my husband who
is in a prison camp. A Sister of the Poor promised to look after them while I was absent, but
she has disappeared as completely as have my
children. I make bold to ask your help, good
Padre, because I cannot think where else to
turn."

"Did you say that your children are three
little girls?" the Padre asked.

She nodded.

"Just step this way, Madame, and look, but
don't say a word." The Padre opened the door
a crack and the woman peeked in. "Are those
the lost children?"

The candlelight falling upon the bed re-
vealed a lovely picture. The woman gave a cry
and leaned against the door, weak with sudden
happiness. After a day and evening of acute
anxiety, the relief of seeing her dear ones, well
and sound, with the calm face of the White

Sister like a guardian angel above them, was more than she could bear.

"Why didn't I come to you at first, Senor Porko?" she exclaimed. "How many hours of heart-ache it would have saved. But what in the world are my children wearing?" The woman was commencing to laugh. "I never saw them look so funny."

The Padre, always bashful before ladies, was now genuinely confused. "Well, you see . . . you see . . . they came here directly from the woods. And of course they did not have their . . . er . . . night things. My pajamas are a trifle large around the neck and waist, especially for the littlest one. And short in the arms. Mrs. Hedge-Hog made them smaller with safety-pins and by tying knots. Now that you speak of it, they do look sort of bunchy, don't they? Especially the girl in my red woolen ones."

The mother burst into a hearty laugh, which was just what she needed, and it was in this

spirit of gaiety that the family was reunited,
thanks to the good Padre. The story of everyone's trials and escapes, which now included
the mother's secret talks by night with her
husband, through the iron fence of the prisoner's camp, had to be told all over again.

Meanwhile the Padre, who never forgot his stomach for very long, had been busy at the fireplace. Now he interrupted the stream of conversation. "Anyone who would like some tomato soup, with crackers to break up in it, raise her right hand. Ah, I thought so," he said with a grunt of satisfaction. "I'm glad I made a lot. But be careful to blow it. It's awfully hot." For five minutes there was no sound but the clicking of spoons.

The mother spoke first. "Our cottage is not very large, but the White Sister can be quite comfortable and safe in our attic. No soldier would ever look there for her."

"There is my garret, too," added the Padre. "But we can believe that the fighting will soon be over, when no one will bother her any more."

"I'm so happy," sighed the middle-sized girl, leaning back upon the pillow, and closing her eyes. "Last night we had no mama. Tonight we have two mamas. And soon we shall have two mamas and a papa." The White Sister and the mother made a bed of blankets and quilts in the corner and lay down.

"What a day it has been," said the Padre, arranging the cushions of his chair, and fumbling in the dark with his buttons. "What a day! It ended with a roaring bull, but it began with so small a thing as a bee."

The Jokes of
SINGLE-TOE

Chestnuts are ripening and falling on the other side of the canal," said the black-headed sparrow, teetering on the edge of the table.

"Oh, but it's too early for chestnuts," objected the Padre. "It takes two or three frosty nights to open the prickles."

"Well, if you can't believe me," said the sparrow, ruffling his collar, "ask the squirrel. He keeps track of the nuts."

So the Padre asked Single-Toe (so named because he had only one on his left front foot). The squirrel put his paw beside his nose as though he were trying to think up an answer to a riddle. "I'll try to let you know in three days," he mumbled, "but don't do anything about chestnuts until you see me again." And he went off in such a rush that even the good Padre grew suspicious.

An hour later he laid down his pipe and beckoned to Mrs. Wren. "Do you mind having a little fly around the wood to see what the squirrel family is up to this morning?"

She came back twittering all over. "The squirrels, for miles around, are all in the grove across the canal, throwing down the chestnuts for dear life. Single-Toe is making them work all the harder, and giggling at something he seems to think very funny."

"Oh, the rascal," chuckled the Padre. "The sly little one-toed sinner! He will give me an answer in three days, will he? Yes, indeed, after he has gathered all the best nuts." He called to his housekeeper. "Mrs. Hedge-Hog, bring me three of the oatmeal sacks from the cupboard and some strong string." And folding the bags inside his belt, he trotted off, pushing his wheelbarrow.

Up among the leaves, busy pulling the polished nuts out of the burrs, Single-Toe and his relatives did not hear the Padre arrive. Patter, plop, plop, plop, patter—the brown nuts were falling on the grass.

"What a lark," beamed the Padre, stuffing four or five into his mouth at once. "And this year they are sweeter and juicier than they have been for a long time." He made little piles of the biggest ones, and began filling his sacks. Finally he had all the wheelbarrow would carry. Bouncing the last bag up and down so he could tie the string around the top, he called out in his silkiest voice, "Many thanks, Single-Toe. You will see that I have taken only the big ones. I do hope that the prickers haven't made your paws sore."

There was a sudden calm in the chestnut grove. The squirrels came leaping down to a

low bough, from where they could send sour
looks after the Padre, trundling his barrow
along toward the bridge. He was singing,

> With chestnuts roasting in a row,
> I love to hear them sizzle.
> I care not how the winds may blow,
> Nor how the rain-drops drizzle.
> I welcome every Jack and Jill
> Who knocks upon my door.
> We toast our toes and eat our fill,
> For there are plenty more.

One day three or
four weeks later the
Padre was doing a
little carpentering
under the umbrella
pine, when some-

thing behind him sniffed. He jumped, and dropped two nails out of his mouth. There, under the table, tears running down their noses, were Mrs. Single-Toe and the four children.

"Bless my blue-eyed buttons," exclaimed the Padre, spitting out the rest of the nails. "What can be as wrong as all that?"

"It's Papa," said the oldest boy. "He's been in a hole by the old oak for four days, and is almost starved."

"But why doesn't he come home?" said the Padre. "The oak isn't far away."

"The fox won't let him," sobbed Madame Single-Toe.

"And why not?"

"He's mad because of Papa's jokes," the youngest child explained.

The Padre's mouth opened in a wide grin. "More of the jokes that other people don't find funny, eh? Well, I'll take a stroll by the twisted oak and have a talk with the fox." As he started off, he called over his shoulder, "Mrs. Hedge-Hog, you might give these youngsters a couple of the pickled chestnuts we keep for company." He winked solemnly at Mrs. Single-Toe, who blushed.

The fox was lying with his muzzle just an inch from the hole. He did not budge, nor lift his eye when the Padre wished him good morning. "I've got him this time," he snarled. "Four days I've been watching this hole. My mother brings my meals and keeps guard while I eat. He'll not get away *this* time!"

"He is a nuisance with his jokes, I admit," said the Padre peaceably, "but he doesn't do any real harm. Don't you think a good scare would be enough for him?"

"No, I don't," snapped the fox. "And don't you mix in this business, Padre, with your talk about kindness. What I've suffered from that little pest you'd never believe. First he dropped a tomato on my nose—a tomato that was too ripe. And then he dribbled pitch all over my head and neck while I was asleep. So don't waste your time." The fox advanced his red tongue hungrily to the very edge of the hole.

The Padre walked away, deep in thought. His generous heart was very unhappy. What should he say to the near-orphans in his kitchen? There must be some way to save him. Suddenly he saw some crows gossiping in a dead pine. "Will one of you black boys do me a favor, in a great hurry?" he called.

"Certainly, Don Porko," they all cawed.

"Fly low through the woods, and tell every rabbit you see that I want their road commissioner to come to my house for dinner. Say that I'm going to have celery root and cabbage, chopped in parsley."

The Padre's guest was promptness itself. He used a turnip leaf as a napkin, and when he had wiped his whiskers, ate the napkin. "It makes less for Ma'am Hedge-Hog to clear up," he explained.

"Now for serious business," said the Padre, leading the way to the garden, when they had finished their second glass of dandelion wine. "I have invited you here as an expert. We will draw a map." He made a cross in the soft earth with a stick. "Here is the oak that the lightning split. And here in front of it, so, is a rabbit hole that was begun, but never finished. Do you follow me?"

The road commissioner nodded. "I know it perfectly. The workman was caught by an owl when he came up with some dirt."

"Now," continued the Padre, "how far is the bottom of this unfinished hole from one of your regular tunnels, and how long would it take to dig up to it?"

"About half a jump," replied the road commissioner. "The 'Alley to the Ivy Rock' runs very close to that unfinished hole. A good digger can do a medium-sized jump of tunnel in half a day. I should say it would take two hours to dig upwards from 'Ivy Rock Alley' and join the hole."

The Padre beckoned the road commissioner to follow him to the cellar. Scraping away the sand, he laid bare ten carrots, each as smooth and straight as an orange-colored candle. "These are yours, Mr. Commissioner, if you will do this little job of digging for me."

The bargain was soon struck. "One thing more," said the Padre, as the commissioner was lolloping away. "You will find a friend of mine in the unfinished hole. Don't let him make a noise, but bring him here the moment you can get him free. I'll be waiting."

Daylight was fading when the rabbit re- turned, covered with damp earth to his armpits. He was supporting a hoarse, hun- gry, and grimy red squirrel. The Padre welcomed them, pointing to the cupboard. "Sh-h-h-sh, go and see what's inside, Single-Toe."

One might have thought a hundred squir- rels were behind the cupboard door, such was the hugging and chattering, the rubbing of noses, and the scratching of ears. Single-Toe was invited to stay for a light lunch, even after the road commissioner had left for his burrow, the biggest carrot in his mouth.

Safe, fed, and warmed, the red squirrel be- came his own gay self again. He began to chuckle, then to shake with merriment. "Ha, ha, ha! That silly old fox is still there, watching an empty hole! Won't it be a priceless joke, if I climb the oak and drop a rotten egg on his nose?"

At the word "joke," Mrs. Single-Toe, the four little squirrels, and the good Padre, all stiffened.

"Don't you ever say that word again," said his wife. "Do you hear, no more jokes, never, never."

Single-Toe wilted. "Yes," he confessed, not daring to meet the Padre's eye, "jokes aren't always so terribly funny, are they? Not even for the joker."

The New-Moon
MEETING

he Padre's cheeks were all puckered to blow out his candle, when a squishy plop was heard on the other side of the door. It was as though someone had dropped a stone into soft mud. Then another plop, but less heavy.

"It's strange how callers always come just when I'm ready for bed," the Padre murmured to himself, setting down the candlestick. "But whoever they are, there are two of them."

He called through the door, "Who is there?"

A rusty gurgle came from close to the ground. "It is the Senior Warden of the Toad Family, Your Honor, and a junior member. Will you kindly let us speak to you?"

Padre Porko swung open the door. "Come in, come in, Warden. You are always welcome." He put the candlestick on the floor, where it was on a level with the toads' heads. Like rubies, their eyes reflected the flame.

"And what might be on your mind this evening?" the Padre asked. "What's wrong among your ancient and honorable tribe?"

The toad spoke with an effort. "Please excuse my voice being hoarse, Chief, for I haven't made a speech in years. Our motto, as you know, is 'Deeds, Not Words.' But perhaps we have carried it too far. At any rate, some of our younger members think we haven't talked enough about ourselves. Everyone knows that we are one of the oldest families among animals, and one of the wisest. But we are old-fashioned; we work hard, never quarrel, never take a vacation. And we work in the night, when no one sees us. As a result, we never get any thanks. Our young folks think it's time we did. But I'll let one of them speak for himself. Warty, it's your turn."

To tell the truth, the young toad had been properly brought up, and was shy about speaking freely before the renowned Padre Porko. However, what he considered the rightness of his cause gave him confidence. He held up the middle finger of his right hand, in an impressive gesture.

"Honored Padre, we are willing to work in the dark, keeping flower gardens clean for other people to enjoy, but we want some appreciation. The birds talk about themselves, and people can see the useful things that cows and horses and poultry do. But no one sees us. No one admires us." Warty wiggled the long finger, to drive home his point.

The Padre leaned back in his chair, his face sympathetic. He was enjoying this. The corner of his mouth twitched in a smile. "What you say, both of you, is more than true. I've often felt that our modest workers are not rewarded enough. But I'm sure that you had some practical plan in mind. What is it?"

The young toad glanced at the Warden for encouragement and then spoke shyly. "We do have a plan. You know the meetings that Your Honor holds at the time of each new moon, when you teach us the animal laws and praise those who are doing well. Well, we would like to ask that you make the next one an 'Honor the Toads' meeting."

The Padre's eyes closed, and he stroked his third chin thoughtfully. From his expression, his thoughts were genial. "No objection to that. None at all," he replied at last. "I like the idea, and I'll do more than you ask. You can arrange the whole program. There will have to be a committee, of course, and since it's Warty's idea, he can be chairman. There will be only one restriction. When the news gets about, other families may want to join in with you. And if they seem to deserve it, you will have to let them be on the committee."

"That's perfectly all right," agreed Warty, with a grin that seemed to split the whole front of his body. "It will be nice to have others behind our movement. The more the merrier."

"I hope you find it so," said the Padre.

"As always, you have been most kind," said the Senior Warden. "Now I must get back to the garden. Right now I'm giving full time to those sow-bugs that nip off roots. My people are the only ones who can handle them. Their shells are so thick that even the blackbirds can't digest them."

"I'm off to spread the good news," warbled Warty. "A thousand thanks, Don Porko."

Goodnights having been said, the good Padre did, at last, blow out his candle.

After a refreshing night, Padre Porko was seated upon the garden bench, and had no more than lighted his after-breakfast pipe, when a dusty shadow flitted from the rose arbor to the seat beside him. The lizard was so excited that the loose skin under his chin puffed out like a balloon.

"I can see it's something special, Squirmy," said the Padre good-naturedly. "Let's have it."

"Oh that I should have lived to see this day!" wept the lizard, standing on his hind legs and wringing his hands. "I wouldn't believe it until I heard that toad Warty say it with his own mouth. I'm sure you didn't mean it, Don Porko, but you have put a slight upon the whole Lizard Family!"

A puzzled wrinkle had appeared upon the

Padre's pink, piggy face, a wrinkle which now moved downward into a smile. He was beginning to guess the nature of Squirmy's trouble.

The lizard slapped his tail on the bench angrily. "They work in the cool of the evening, those toads, while we lizards broil in the blazing sun. They take the big, tasty mouthfuls like the June bugs and May flies, while we take the little pests, which make you scramble all day to get a meal—the mites, gnats, and mosquitoes. You've never had a screen on your house, Chief, nor needed one, because we lizards were on watch for your comfort. But have we ever asked for recognition? Yet today the toads are singing that all the creatures of earth and sky, led by the great Padre Porko himself, are going to have a meeting to honor them. Imagine it! Not one word about the lizards."

The Padre drew on his pipe thoughtfully. "Would it make you feel better if you had a part in the program?" he asked. "And if you yourself were a member of the committee?"

"Of course it would, Chief!" cried Squirmy.

"Then go and tell Warty that, as agreed, the lizards are to have a member on the committee."

Before the sun had set that evening, the Padre had been approached by delegations from three other tribes of little people whose pride had been hurt by the news. One and all, the ants, the bees, and the beetles buzzed the same indignation—that a new-moon meeting should be devoted only to the toads.

To each delegation the Padre made the same reply. "My friends, I sympathize with you. Tell young Warty that you are members of the program committee." And as each group of delighted workers set out to find the toad chairman, the Padre would take one of the skippy little dance steps that he made when affairs were marching nicely.

It was now forty-eight hours since the first visit of the toads, and Padre Porko was at home, awaiting the report of the committee. Warty was strangely depressed. He squatted down, exhausted. From much wrangling, his voice, never strong at best, had about disappeared.

"We acted hastily," he whispered hoarsely. "I wish I'd never started this thing. It's out of control, Your Honor. It won't be a meeting, but a three-day convention."

The Padre looked sympathetic. "What's the trouble, Warty? Too many events?"

"That's just it, Chief. I had a nice poem to

open with—*Ode to a Toad*—but Squirmy insists upon reading his poem, too. The bees have a song seven pages long. The ants have charades on ants in the Bible. The beetles have borrowed an illustrated lecture." He paused to scowl at Squirmy. "There's bound to be a fight. And I know one lizard that'll lose his tail."

Squirmy took the floor. "Then there's the matter of the name. It can't be called an 'Honor the Toads' meeting, because now the lizards are in it. Therefore I propose that it be called 'Honor the Anti-Insect Tribes.' "

At once there was a tempest of feverish small sounds. "Never, never, none of that anti-insect talk! Only over our dead bodies!" The bees were swarming in the air, buzzing angrily. The ants were lining up in battle formation, sharpening their pincers against one another. The beetles had disappeared, but from the nervous glances Squirmy threw behind him, he had a good idea as to where they were.

The confusion was at its height, when a low, liquid whistle sounded outside. The Padre went to the door. A brown and orange shell was balanced on the step.

"My soul and body," exclaimed the good Padre, "if it isn't Old Century himself."

The land tortoise did not enter, but spoke through the opening. "We have just had word that a testimonial is being given for careful and quiet workmen. I have come to request a place on the program."

"Oh, oh, oh," buzzed and rasped everyone. "This is positively the last straw!" With a single mind they began to hop, run, and fly toward the nearest door or window. As he hopped out, Warty croaked, "I wash my hands of it, Don Porko."

With the last one gone and the door latched, the Padre laughed and laughed until the tears trickled down his nose.

However, the new-moon meeting did take

place, and it was truly a success. As the different clans, homeward bound, threaded their ways through the forest, the air was full of exclamations of pleasure. Everyone was talking at once.

"Wasn't that sweet about the bees being the voices of the flowers?"

"The round dance of the lizards was perfectly timed, wasn't it?"

"And the Padre's speech was just right, too. A real tribute to all the silent workers who are doing their tasks well, not for praise, but because each is part of Mother Nature's plan."

A gossipy lizard spoke up. "But where were the toads? Not one of them showed up."

"Well, you see," explained the Padre, "the toads have never been used to talking, and they debated so much about what they should or shouldn't do, that they lost their voices completely. None of them could make a sound. And anyway, their motto is 'Deeds, Not Words,' you know."

The OUTLAW

The jolliest party of the year was the Padre's Wood-Gathering. It was always held on a Sunday, so that the working animals could come. And it came at the end of summer, when the branches which had fallen from the trees would be brittle and easy to break.

On Wood-Gathering Day, the Padre always issued strict orders that, from one hour before daylight until one hour after sunset, no animal should hurt any other animal. That was so that everyone could wear his best clothes and travel fearlessly in the middle of the road. It was one day on which the foxes and the geese, the dogs and the rabbits, the cats and the field mice, the hawks and the sparrows must be helpful and polite to one another.

There were many kinds of work—something for everyone. First, the pulling down and the breaking up of the twigs and boughs. The oxen could crack even big wood just by stepping on it. Among the low trees the goats were very clever. They would stand on their hind legs, hook their horns over a branch, give a sharp yank, and down would tumble stick and goat together. The squirrels stayed in the trees, working as partners with the goats. For when a bough was too thick for the goat's weight to break, a couple of good squirrel bites would weaken it. The stick would barely touch the ground before it was seized by some beak or mouth and carried to the central wood pile.

The hardest job was to tie the pieces into bundles. Here the snakes were wonderful. Judge Fork-Tongue and his family would wind themselves around a jumble of branches, tightening their gray bodies until everything was squeezed into a neat packet. Meanwhile a nimble rat would be drawing a vine around the bundle, and tucking in the end to make a knot. Back and forth trotted the donkeys, carrying the finished bundles under shelter. The rabbits brought in the vines that served as cords. The birds flew back and forth as messengers.

Of course, the high spot of the day was the picnic under the umbrella pine. The Widow Hedge-Hog had her three sisters and nine of her nieces in for the day to help with the cooking. There had to be three tables, to suit the three kinds of appetites. The simplest was for the snakes, toads, lizards, and turtles, for they wanted only tepid milk, sweetened with honey. The meal for the largest animals began with oatmeal, then came piles and piles of sweet-smelling clover hay, with tender, juicy green leaves for dessert. The table for mixed ap-

petites was by far the largest, for it included
the birds, who liked a dab of everything. The
main dishes for this table were vegetable salad
and cooked carrots and potatoes, topped off
with berries and nuts. And there was plenty of
honey for all who wanted it. The Padre had
asked his bees to make an extra effort, and
they had produced enough flower honey to
glue together the feathers and fur of the whole
forest.

When every plate had been licked, nibbled,
and pecked clean, Professor Stork proposed a
vote of thanks to the cooks. The birds sang
three numbers, and then the picnickers folded
their paws over their stomachs or tucked their
heads under their wings and settled down for a
nice after-dinner nap.

But the peaceful sleepers were rudely
awakened by a growling "wuff-wuff-wuff."
Smashing the young trees, pushing down the
bushes, a shaggy head rose among the ferns.

Sniffing hungrily, it approached the tables.

None of the Padre's animals had ever imagined such a creature. "It's a kangaroo," cried some. "It's a buffalo," cried others.

"No," said the Padre, hastily buttoning his velvet jacket, "it's a bear. He's a foreigner and he doesn't know Spanish ways, but he looks as though somebody had been giving him a rough time. Just sit quiet while I find what he wants."

The gaunt animal that limped toward the picnickers was indeed a grimy sight. He was all bones. A collar, now gone, had worn the hair from his neck. The bare spots on his skin were muddy and raw.

The Padre saw at once that this was a guest whose appetite was not to be trifled with. It was a delicate moment, too, for the bear was slyly edging toward a plump lady goat. To defend her, the Padre stepped gallantly between her and the newcomer, then stopped, horrified and shivering. Was he not himself a juicy temptation to put within reach of a starving stranger?

But Padre Porko kept his presence of mind. With a quick side step, he spread a rug, invited the visitor to be seated, and called to the cooks to hustle along whatever might be left in the kitchen. To fill the time, he invited the traveller to tell his story, for who doesn't like to talk about himself?

"I was born in Hungary," growled the bear, "and I'm trying to get away from a gypsy circus, where they starved and abused me. I heard about you, and figured this would be a good place to hide and rest for a few days."

"My small house is always open to all animals in trouble," replied the Padre, with one of his gentlemanly bows. "Oh, but I'm forgetting the honey. We keep a spare jar in the cellar. Bears do like honey, don't they?" He trotted off and soon returned with a three-quart bowl, full to the brim, which he set before the uninvited guest.

Looking to neither right nor left, the bear buried his muzzle and sucked greedily. Eyes shut, he did not appear to breathe until the bowl was empty. And while he lost the fierce edge of his hunger as the honey went down, he also lost the end of such good manners as he may once have possessed.

"That was all right as an appetizer, Funny-Face, but now get busy with the real meal." The bear yawned, disclosing his rows of sharp yellow teeth. "I'm going to like this place. Nice garden. Fruit getting ripe. No men. Quite a few beehives. Lots of fat, tender little friends running in and out." He leered at the picnickers, showing his teeth again. "Running *in,* that is. Ha, ha! Yes, I've found a nice little place to pass my old age." Suddenly he turned ugly. "Listen here, Pink-Eye! Do I have to tell you again; where's my dinner?"

The animals of the picnic were paralyzed. No man or beast had ever yet made fun of their

Padre Porko. He was the cleverest person on earth, and no one would think of addressing him disrespectfully. But the Padre had not lost his temper. Even when the vulgar foreigner was guzzling down food as fast as the Widow Hedge-Hog, her sisters, and her nine nieces could fetch it out, the Padre's courtly manner did not change.

At last the bear patted his full stomach. "I tell you what we'll do, old Moon-Face," he growled. "We'll get more cooks. We'll need ten or twenty more. And while I think of it, have your people bring a few loads of dry grass into the cellar. I'll fix a little bed for myself until the gypsies have left this part of Spain. And have a good hot supper at five o'clock. I guess I'll have a bit of a snooze while you get my room in order." He curled his long back into a ball and was soon snoring.

The distressed friends of the Padre stood around, nervously wondering what they could

do to help Don Porko be rid of so dangerous a
visitor. It was Judge Fork-Tongue who offered
a solution.

"I've always said, Chief," he hissed, "that
you are too big-hearted, too easy-going. And
this time you've caught a Tartar. This fellow's
meaner than poison. You'll have nothing but
trouble with him. He's a criminal, and no one
hereabouts can handle him except my son and
I. While he's asleep we'll take a strangle hold
around his throat that'll shut his windpipe like
a piece of wire. He'll never know what got him.
Say the word, Padre, and it's as good as done."

But Padre Porko shook his head. "Sorry, Judge, but I can't. I've given my word. This bear has been living with men so long that he has forgotten how animals should act."

Then began some very unhappy weeks for the Widow Hedge-Hog and her employer. Each day the bear grew more exacting. He found fault with everything. He complained that the food lacked variety, that the oatmeal was always burned, that there were leaves in the blueberries, that the sun bothered his sore eyes, that the singing of the tree toads kept him awake. He would take the dishes from the table and empty them down his throat, leaving nothing for the Padre. He ate between meals. The baskets of beets, onions, chestnuts, and turnips, that were to be the whole winter's supply, were emptying fast. One morning the Padre even found a beehive tipped over and smashed, with the wax and honey scooped out, and the bees scattered and scared.

The afternoon of that same day, as the Padre was untying a package of groceries that Sobersides, the donkey, had just brought from the store, a headline in the newspaper wrapping caught his eye:

Goliath, Giant Cinnamon Bear
of the Royal Zoo, Madrid, Is Dead.

Telling the donkey to wait, Padre Porko climbed to the attic and threw down the lumber that he had been saving to build a summerhouse. From the woodshed he got hammer, saw, wire, and nails. What he then put together was a long, strong box, bound round and round with wire. Single-Toe, the squirrel, handed up the nails. Sobersides, the donkey, pulled the wire so tight that it sang, while the Padre fastened the staples. Now and then the three workers would stare at one another and wink.

At four o'clock, yawning and arching his sleek back, the bear came sleepily from the cel-

lar. "What are you building, old Flop-Ear?
Your hammering woke me an hour too soon.
Don't let it happen again." He licked his lips.
"Whew, but I'm thirsty."

"This is my patented model beehive," said
the Padre. "Our hives are much too small, and
don't hold enough honey. I'm leaving the door
open so that the bees will get acquainted with
their new home."

The bear's nose was in the air, sniffing, trying to locate some delicious smell. He pushed
his head through the door of the model hive.
"What's in that pail at the other end?"

"Oh, that's nothing," replied the Padre care-
lessly, driving home the last nail. "Only some
honey and water to draw the bees in."

"Honey and water!" snorted the thirsty bear.
"Do you mean to say you'd give honey and
water to those lazy little beggars? Let them
gather their own honey. My throat's as dry as
pepper."

The big brown body squeezed inside the box, and the bear's head disappeared in the pail, sucking noisily. Sobersides, his four feet braced, was pushing the door shut with all his strength. The Padre was screwing down the nuts that fastened the door. The birds and squirrels, who had been assembling in answer to the mysterious news that something terrific was about to happen at the Padre's, nearly fell out of the umbrella pine with excitement, when the first stupendous howl rose from the model beehive. Like a toy boat in a flood, the box creaked and rolled. The watchers thought it would never be strong enough, or big enough, to contain the fury that was roaring and snapping inside. But the planks of oak did not crack. The wires that Sobersides had drawn tight held fast. And when the bear had worn himself out, Padre Porko spoke through a knothole.

"We are sorry to do this, but it is for your

own good. You have stolen from men, and three of them with guns are hunting you. If you stay here you will be shot. But where you are going you will have plenty to eat. Thousands will admire you every day. You will never have to get up early in the morning. Isn't that just your kind of life for a happy old age?"

Gradually the snarls quieted to a rumbly-mumbly chorus of grunts. At bottom the bear was a philosopher. Life had brought him many ups and downs. And before the stars came out,

the outlaw was asleep, ready for the next adventure.

Farmer Edwardo's ox-cart unloaded a long box at the railway station. The station-master whistled when he saw what was inside.

"How'd you catch him?" he enquired. "And where's he going?"

"Climb up and have a look for yourself," replied Edwardo with a grin. "There's a card on top."

The station-master fished out his spectacles and read:

For the Manager

Royal Zoo, Madrid

Donated by P. Porko and Friends